Mending Defects

Also by Lynn Galli

Wasted Heart

Imagining Reality

Uncommon Emotions

Blessed Twice

Full Court Pressure

Finally

Mending Defects

Lynn Galli

Penikila Press

Chapter 1

I was shoveling the last third of my driveway when I noticed an unfamiliar woman emerge from the house closest to mine. She waved at the big truck in her drive as it rumbled to life and pulled away. I hadn't paid much attention to it because the McGraths were always changing out the furniture in their winter home. Even from a distance, I could tell this woman wasn't a McGrath. Without the massive staff of minions to order around, she couldn't be a designer either.

When I got back inside, a message on my answering machine satisfied my curiosity. The McGraths had sold their home, or so my realtor friend told me. I wasn't sure how to feel about that. As tourists, the McGraths never stayed longer than a couple months a year. For the rest of the time, my quiet corner of the neighborhood stayed noise, traffic, and chitchat free.

I sighed, knowing I should go introduce myself. I haven't had to do that in years, but it was the neighborly thing to do. Maybe I should make something. There weren't many restaurants open nearby on a Sunday night and no one remembers to label the box with the coffeemaker. Yeah, I should put something together.

Not knowing what she liked, I decided on quick and easy staples. I made some sandwiches, soup, added half the pasta salad I was having for dinner, and wrapped up the banana and zucchini breads I'd made this afternoon. If all that failed, she'd hopefully appreciate the fresh coffee I added to a thermos. Picnic basket now full, I went into the mudroom to gear up in Sorels, a parka, mittens, and a ski hat before I could head back outside.

Snow fell in a light dusting still, making the air feel heavy. Out on the street, I took stock of my neighborhood. Smoke curled up into the white sky from my friend Spencer's house. Across the way and up from his place, Nancy and Calvin's house glowed bright enough to be seen from space. Neither of them had given advance warning of a new neighbor, which was surprising since Nancy liked to think that nothing happened in this neighborhood without her knowing. As it was, she'd probably spent her afternoon with binoculars trying to track every movement at the former house of McGrath.

Halfway to the new neighbor's house, I paused to catch my breath, setting the basket down. Cold weather always did this to me. Like a punch to the gut, it could stop me dead. My heart constantly struggled to pump blood through my body in winter. It would be smarter to move to a warmer climate, but I wouldn't let a heart condition force me out of this beautiful ski town. I'd learned to work around it with lots of breaks and slower movements.

Ten minutes later, I landed on the McGrath's porch. Knocking went unnoticed. I hoped she wasn't trying to massage away her moving aches in the bathtub. No way would she accept a picnic basket sitting on her stoop without first meeting the basket giver, but I didn't have the energy for a roundtrip back to my house to pick up a notepad. I should have planned this better.

While I was beating myself up, I heard a soft noise from inside. The curtains in the front window fell back into place, and after a long delay, the door opened. Cracked would be more accurate, just far enough to show a sliver of that face that had drawn my interest from afar.

Up close, it was captivating. Rich skin tone, darker than most pale folks around here. My German-Irish self looked ghostly after a full winter. This woman didn't have that problem. With brown, almond shaped eyes set at an angle, her skin tone wasn't the only alluring thing about her. Prominent cheekbones and a fine nose distinguished her beautiful triangular face as unique. Her long hair in a shade between brown and black was slicked back into a thick braid. At roughly five-seven, she was tall compared to my sixty-two inches. Fit, too, which was a nice change from the typical tourist twiggy. She had muscle definition under her silk turtleneck and strong thighs encased in comfortable jeans. She wouldn't be snapping any bones putting on her ski boots.

I realized I'd been staring too long and flipped on my neighborly smile. I was going for harmless, although I'd settle for looking like I hadn't poisoned my food. "Hi, I'm Glory Eiben, your neighbor just down the road." I turned and pointed toward my house, only part of which could be seen through the trees. "Welcome. I noticed the movers leaving and thought I'd come introduce myself."

Her head tilted, eyes narrowing. After an interminable moment, she smiled and opened the door wide. "Hi, Glory, I'm Lena." Her voice was as rich as her skin tone. It moved like honey out of a jar, oozing over the space between us.

We stared at each other, me not knowing if that constituted an invite inside, and her probably shocked at having a neighbor show up on her doorstep. We did things a little differently here in Aspen. If she was from a big city, she'd probably think I was pulling a prank on her.

I held up my picnic basket. "I brought some food to tide you over until your kitchen's unpacked."

She scrutinized the proffered basket. Time slowed under her careful examination. Bomb sniffing dogs weren't this thorough. Finally satisfied, she stepped back, waving me inside.

"Thank you." She reached out to take it from my hands. Her arm dipped, having underestimated the reason I was using two hands. "What's in here?" She looked down at the offending basket as we strolled farther inside.

I laughed and those alluring eyes blinked several times before refocusing with intent. "I figured you hadn't been grocery shopping yet, and you won't find many restaurants open about now."

"If you tell me there's coffee in here, I'll worship you forever." She slid the basket onto the marble countertops the McGraths had installed years before they were fashionable.

"There's coffee in there."

Her eyes grew larger, a wide smile touching her full lips. Beautiful and so not right that she'd just moved in next to me. She'd taunt me with her perfect, no doubt straight self every day until some other tourist decided that wintering in Aspen was an absolute must.

"You'll have to wait until I unpack my shrine supplies."

Such a dry delivery, I almost didn't know if she was kidding. We both turned to look at the multitude of boxes scattered around the big open layout. It was a lot of stuff for a winterer.

"Need some help unpacking?" I heard myself offer. Something must have taken over my brain. This would take all night even with both of us, and I barely had the energy left to walk back home.

A soft laugh pulsed from her lips. I must not be the only one who thought my offer was crazy. "No, thanks, I'll get to it all."

I nodded, glancing around to take in the tasteful furniture. "Are you familiar with Aspen or do you need a map? I'd be happy to draw one up with all the exciting spots."

She checked her watch. "You mean the ones that close down by seven o'clock?"

I both resented the jab and loved the biting tone. She'd be fun to have as a friend, but her guarded look told me she wasn't looking for any new friends. She was in for a huge surprise. Small town life made it so she'd gain new friends whether she wanted them or not. She'd only have to deal with it while she was vacationing, but she'd get those unwanted friends.

"At least one of the bars stays open till midnight on Saturdays," I countered with a smile.

"Let me guess; it closes at midnight because the bars aren't open on Sundays?"

"You *are* familiar with Aspen." I joked about the abandoned practice in town. At one time, Aspen had been just a ski town. Now it was a resort destination that garnered the interest of some of the wealthiest people and celebrities in the world. Old time rules had to be updated as the town changed.

"I was kidding, but I see you're not. God, what have I let myself in for?" She seemed to be talking to herself, but her words made me second guess her tenure here.

"You're not a winter wonderer, are you?"

"Pardon?" Suspicion entered her gaze.

"Someone who winters here or only comes for the skiing?"

She paused, making me feel like I shouldn't have asked such a personal question, even if it wasn't that personal. "No, I'm not."

A permanent neighbor. This I liked even less than I'd liked the idea of the McGraths no longer living here. That she wasn't the friendliest puppy in the litter made the situation all the more awkward. "Then I really mean the welcome wishes. Before I was just being polite. Now I want to get on your good side."

She chuckled again, sizing me up. "An oddball, how refreshing. Didn't think I'd find one in such a small town."

"The oddest," I confirmed, not at all insulted.

"Good to know." She lifted the top of the picnic basket and peered inside. "Tell me you're a good cook, and I'll carve a statue of you to go in the worship corner."

"I'm a good baker."

She plucked up the zucchini bread and brought it to her nose for a long sniff. Bliss took over her expression. My mind went straight to the notion that this might be her afterglow face. Such a wrong thought when meeting my beautiful, straight, permanent, straight, statuesque, yet still straight, neighbor.

"Seems like," she said between sniffs. "It's a big promise. I have a thirty-five point rating scale when it comes to baked goods."

"Only thirty-five? Not very particular, are you?" I grinned and caught the one she tried to hide by looking at the piles of boxes surrounding us. There really were a lot of them. I should help her. My neighbors all liked each other. I needed the same from this woman. "Please let me help you unpack. This looks like it will take you weeks."

Her glance sharpened. "I'm fine, thanks."

So much for trying to be neighborly. "The offer stands. I'm usually around in the evenings. I'd be glad to help you get rid of the boxes or restock your bakery section. Just let me know."

Her nod wasn't as curt as I expected, but she did start toward the front door. "It was nice of you to bring over the basket. I hadn't counted on this as a benefit of moving to a small town."

"We are very Mayberry at times," I said, following her.

She laughed again and I paused. Nice laugh, short, breathy, and genuine. "I caught on when I stopped off at the gas station outside of town and got everything but a heat lamp with the interrogation."

Now her guarded stance made sense. Small towns could be a little annoying to newcomers. A little annoying to current residents, too, but newcomers were especially assaulted by the we-will-find-out-everything-about-you-we-have-our-ways attitude.

"If you can make it past the initial curiosity phase, you'll be interrogation free. After that, everyone will just think they know everything about you." I'd benefited from this small town practice my entire adult life.

"I'll be looking forward to that." She reached for the doorknob.

I admired her superpower. Deflection would suit her well here. I hadn't learned anything about her other than her name and fondness for coffee and baked items. Oh, and she was independent, didn't like to accept help, and wasn't used to small towns. On the whole, I'd learned a lot, but not the stuff that I was sure everyone else in town would want to know about her.

"It was nice meeting you, Lena. If there's anything you need or you decide the woods around you sound too quiet, like I said, I'm just up the road a bit. Come on by anytime."

"Thanks," she said before closing the door behind me.

A little mystery. I liked that.

From the Journal of Lena Coleridge:

It's as small as I remembered. Maybe smaller, but still breathtakingly beautiful. The mountains seem to be calling to me. This was the right decision. The high school would be like any other school, smaller, but a high school. Only now, when I finish work, I have the beauty of this place to surround me instead of city streets, obnoxious noise, and smoggy air.

One detriment—damn, these people are nosy. No less than five people asked who I was and where I was moving when I stopped off for gas in town. I'm glad I remembered the directions or I would have led them right to me. And my four neighbors, yes, only four on this street, two of whom live in the same house, showed up within the first hour of unpacking.

The retired couple had lots of questions under the guise of polite conversation. They expressed concern after learning I would be living here alone. I should have known it would be too much to hope for the same kind of disinterested, self-involved neighbors I had back in Baltimore.

The guy from the architecturally stunning house up the way seemed nice. Younger by probably five years. With a groomed beard and glasses, it was hard to tell. He let me know he lives in the house alone. Name and marital status must be a standard greeting around here. Right before he left, he mentioned he was the mayor. Of the town. Where I now live. He just happened to mention it, like he was telling me to have a nice day.

My next door neighbor, or as next door as a hundred yards away can be, showed up last. At least she'd given me a full hour to settle in. Sweet girl, well, woman by most standards, but really still a girl, probably mid twenties. Very all-American girl next door look about her, complete with heart shaped face, vivid blue eyes, and shoulder length, strawberry blond hair. Truly strawberry, I'm not making that up. And pretty. Really pretty. Annoying not going to be able to look past it pretty. Genuinely sweet, too. Brought over a picnic basket with enough food to sustain me for a week. Her zucchini bread melted in my mouth and the superb coffee was exactly what I needed. I'd be days from finding all my cooking supplies, and I could never bake like this. Really nice of her, but her repeated offers to help me unpack the house were a little much. No one is that nice. She must have been angling for something. Probably wanted to be the first person to report back to the town elders on the stranger in town.

God, listen to me. I'd better cut this attitude or the years here might be as bad as my last two in Baltimore.

Chapter 2

The classic Victorian, once my business partner's family home in the West End, now served as an office to her investment firm, my best friend's law practice, and my accounting firm. The slate blue house sits on a corner lot three blocks over from Main Street. If it hadn't been purchased by Brooke's grandparents over fifty years ago, we'd never have been able to afford it. Victorians in the West End required oil baron money these days.

I slipped my car into the third space of the detached garage out back. As I emerged, the neighbor's side door opened up and out bounded the fifteen-year-old dynamo known as Ashlyn, star soccer, volleyball, and softball player, national merit scholar, and all around great girl.

"Hiya, Glory!" she called out in a cheery tone. Nothing seemed to get this kid down even with all the pressure she faced as the eldest child in a house that now included a younger brother and two-year-old triplets. She bounded across the long side yard to the small picket fence separating us. "I was going to shovel that berm before I headed to school. Did you have any trouble getting in?"

"Nope, didn't snow as much as they said it would." I glanced at my watch. Still forty-five minutes before school started. I knew she'd have time, but I felt bad that she'd miss out on the socializing before. "Come inside when you're done. I'll give you a ride to school on Slick."

"Outlaw! You'll have time?"

My heart hurt by how much a little attention meant to her. The triplets and her six-year-old brother demanded it all from her parents. I tried not to resent them, but it was getting harder and harder. "Clear it with your mom first. Hey, did Brooke pay you for last week?"

Red appeared on her cheeks. Just as I suspected. Ashlyn had a hard time asking to be paid for the yard work and snow shoveling she did for a lot of neighbors. She ducked into the garage before I could give her another lesson on bill collecting.

"Morning, Hazel," I greeted our office manager when I walked inside.

A short white crown of hair lifted from staring down at her desk. A few months shy of sixty-five, Hazel ran this place as well as the eight-child household she'd run for forty years. "Good morning, Glorious One."

I smiled at the pet name. "Will you do up a check for Ashlyn, please? Big surprise, Brooke forgot on Friday."

She laughed at the dichotomy that was Brooke, expert investment strategist but hopeless with personal finances. Reaching for the firm's checkbook, she said, "Heard you got a new neighbor."

I stopped my advance and turned to face her. She knew? I had no idea how the town network spread news so fast. "Guess so." I didn't comment further. Lena didn't deserve to be the source of gossip.

"Is she a turkey?"

I giggled at Hazel's name for tourists who bought homes to use for two weeks and rented them out for the rest of the ski season. "Not that I could tell."

"You didn't say hello?" She leaned forward over her desk.

"I did, but she was in the middle of unpacking." I left out the part about Lena being a little standoffish. People should form their own opinions about her.

"Hmm," she mused. "Haven't heard anything about her other than the McGraths got an offer they couldn't refuse."

"Been watching *The Godfather* again, Hazel?"

Her eyes twinkled as she let up on the inquisition. No wonder Lena had felt cornered yesterday.

I headed into the kitchen to start some coffee and ran into Brooke. A pen perched on her ear, shooting through the short strands of brown. She'd had lots of hair styles since I'd started working for her in college, but this one suited her best. It highlighted her dark blue eyes and complimented her tapered oval face.

"Hey, Glory. How was your weekend?"

"Great, yours?" I shortened any of our conversations during stock market hours. Until the closing bell, Brooke watched her screens like a Vegas surveillance spotter, surfacing only to grab a cup of tea before heading back up to her command center on the second floor.

"Got in some good skiing. I'll tell you about it later." She tipped her head and rushed out of the kitchen. At forty-four, she could compete with Ashlyn on energy levels. I often got tired just watching her.

I started a fresh pot of coffee and headed back into the foyer to find Ashlyn waiting already. "Let's hit the track, youngster."

Her face, maturing into what I guessed would be striking, broke into a sparkling smile. Dark blond hair that she kept in a permanent ponytail got covered by the knit cap she shoved down over her head at my order. We traipsed out the back door to the storage shed where I kept Slick, my snowmobile. Anything that fun to play with deserved a name.

Helmets on, we took turns straddling the seat. Ashlyn reached forward to grip my waist when I pressed the start button. Revving the engine, I eased out onto the yard, skating along the side of the driveway and onto the street. Riding snowmobiles wasn't legal on public streets in town, but the police let most of the locals get away with it.

A few turns later, I burst into the forest that lined the main highway and slowed to a stop. Ashlyn's hands loosened their grip. She slid back on the seat, thinking she'd crowded me. She was like a lot of people in town, worried about my physical state. It used to bother me, but now I realized it was all part of living here.

"Want to drive?" I asked.

She grinned and practically leapfrogged me to switch places. As soon as my hands locked around her waist, we were off. Two miles whizzed past us before we pulled up to the side of the school. She kicked off the front of the snowmobile and lifted the helmet from her head. "Thanks, Glory. That was a blast."

I tipped my visor up to say goodbye as the first bell rang in the distance. "Have a great day, kiddo."

"See ya." She waved and headed toward the nearest group. They let her catch up before turning as one to go inside.

A lone figure stood out from the rest, long and lean in a business suit that looked both casual and elegant. So out of place for the standard just-came-off-the-mountain faculty attire. She waited with watchful eyes as most kids moved in slow motion toward the start of their school day. Her eyes landed on the one group who'd probably wait until the last second to head inside. Most of the faculty would have ignored them, but she didn't give them any room. Heading straight for them, she called out something from two steps away. The group turned in surprise, not expecting to be challenged. I recognized a few of them. No, they wouldn't expect to be challenged, but within ten seconds, they were headed inside.

Interesting.

When the woman's gaze turned toward me, I straightened on the seat. The new principal. The one who replaced our dearly loved, long tenured principal who'd suffered a massive stroke and passed away two months ago was now in place. Beatrice L. Coleridge, great name, but not why I'd voted for her and mine had been the deciding vote. The school board couldn't decide if it wanted to promote from within or bring in someone from the outside. Her résumé was impressive. I hadn't needed to sit in on the interviews to know she'd be perfect. With my vote, the board moved forward to extend an offer.

I doubted she knew that as she gave me a stern glance. A glance that said it was time to start school and she didn't care if I was a worried parent or a vagrant. I had no business being there once the second bell rang.

It was the same glance she'd given me last night on her doorstep when I'd welcomed her to town.

Chapter 3

Being stared at by toddlers was never fun. Having it occur in a doctor's office that catered to kids didn't make it any less awkward. At least there was a teenager in the waiting room this time, so I wasn't the only giant being stared at today.

"Come on back, Glory," the nurse, whose name was either Sydney or Stacy ended the staring contest I was having with a five-year-old named Jeffrey, or so his mother's repeated warnings to him let me know.

I burst out of my seat, sparking my heart rate into a racing clip. Not the best move when going into a cardiac examination, but I didn't care. I wanted out of this office. It didn't matter that I'd been in this room every year for the past thirteen years. My nerves never got any better no matter how many times I got good news with my annual checkup.

She left me in the room to strip down to the gown. I studied his office while I changed. He'd brought in all new cartoon posters this year. I didn't recognize the characters anymore. Some even had Japanese symbols in the conversation bubbles. Trends change, I guess.

A soft knock on the door heralded my doctor. "How are you doing, Glory?"

"I just out-stared a five-year-old without blinking for two minutes, Doc. Feeling pretty good."

He sat and slid the rolling stool into motion in one movement. "Good competition, no aerobics."

The S nurse came back in and slipped the blood pressure cuff on me. An arm squeeze later, she related the stats to Dr. Pickford.

"Blood pressure's high," he commented.

Damn. That was never good news, but what mattered was the ultrasound.

Dr. Pickford rolled the machine over as the nurse handed him the gel and arranged my gown for the test. The gel was cold as it went on. I never got used to that, but the wand helped warm it up as he pressed down and swiped it over my heart. Grey blobby images appeared on the screen. I could see the shape of my heart and even make out one of the chambers without his assistance. Flashes of red and blue overlaid the grey blob. This gave him my blood flow rate. I tried not to look now that I understood what the colors meant. It kept me from getting worked up at the sight of too much blue.

His head swung back, and he looked right at me. I felt my heart thud. He only looked at me when he had news. "Oxygen levels aren't great. You're at 91%. See here," he said, pointing to a dark thin line surrounded by grey, "one of your stents needs replacing. There's leakage around the sutures in the shunt." He showed the blood flow again and sure enough, lots of blue in that area.

Double damn. It had been eight years since I'd needed a stent. Another five years since I'd had my last open heart surgery. I knew I should be counting my blessings. I'd been reminded of that since I was born, but it didn't make the sick feeling I had in my stomach any better.

"We'll try the femoral artery again." He stepped over to his computer to bring up his schedule.

"Didn't work last time," I muttered as S nurse handed me a wipe to take off the gel.

It amazed me how quickly I became seventeen again whenever he gave me bad news. Not that this was as bad as the news I'd received when I was in high school, but any heart procedure was bad news. After six open heart surgeries and three stent replacements, I'd had my quota of bad news from this man.

"We can use the carotid instead." This he directed to his computer screen. He didn't have to worry about his screen giving him a snarky reply. He knew I'd weigh the options of scarring and pick the femoral. I wanted to avoid adding a second scar near the one that looked like a vampire missing a fang had bitten my neck.

"Can it wait a year?" I asked.

He rotated to face me, sympathy in his eyes. "You must have noticed a drop in your energy levels. It can't wait a year. Three months at the most."

Three months put me smack dab in the middle of summer. As much as I wanted to put off this procedure, I couldn't go through the heat without good oxygenation. This should be an easy decision. It really should, but the worst part about having congenital heart disease was that if you lived long enough, you had to make the hard decisions instead of leaving that to your parents.

"After tax day." I pulled out my phone and checked my schedule to set a date that wouldn't affect my work and allowed me a full week's rest afterward.

"The last one did its job for eight years, Glory. We'll use a covered stent to lessen any leakage in the future."

Yippee. But he didn't need my sarcastic reply. The man was nice enough to keep me and a handful of other adults as patients despite being a pediatric heart specialist. I didn't need to throw sarcasm at him. The other bad thing about having a rare congenital heart defect was that no adult heart surgeon knew as much about my condition as pediatric surgeons. Kids had never lived long enough to be treated as adults. I'd stick with my doctor as long as he'd keep me. He was the reason I was alive, the only reason. He was stuck with me until he kicked my defective heart out. Motivation enough to hold back on my sarcasm.

After deciding on a date, I made goodbye sounds to get out of the office. Outside, I took a long breath. I could feel my heart rate slow. Just getting out of there always helped, but the dread remained. This procedure meant a three hour surgery if everything went well. If they had to try both the femoral and the carotid to go through, I'd be on the table for six or more. A day and night in the hospital would be followed by a week of not exactly comfortable recovery. I wanted to get through tax day and go skiing one last time for the season. It would give me just enough time to psych myself up for this.

The last time I'd gone through this, I'd been on summer break from college. My mom and dad had been by my side. I didn't have to worry about studying or keeping up with anyone on campus. This time, I was a functioning adult, and I couldn't put off my responsibilities for more than a week.

Having half a heart sucked.

You heard me right. Where most people were born with four heart chambers, I'd been born with three, one of which was underdeveloped. Through a series of surgeries, they'd closed off the left side of my heart and built functional pathways in my chambers and vascular system to redirect the flow of blood to work with a two chamber heart. Unfortunately, the shunt, valves, arteries, and veins were overworked, which required some reinforcement from time to time. This was one of those times.

Another deep breath later, my head tilted toward the sky. The sun was shining today, but it was still very cold. My breath plumed out in front of me. I was alive. Anyone born with this condition a year or two before me would have died before they reached the age of one, some within weeks.

So, I needed a new stent. I was alive at the age of thirty when my parents had been told I'd be lucky to make it a year, then three, then six, then past my teens. Once I'd broken through my teens with a new valve, I was granted longevity. As long as I followed a healthy lifestyle and stayed within my limits, minor tune-ups should be all I had to face. I was grateful. This stent wouldn't take me down.

"Hi, sweetie." My mom picked up on the first ring. "How'd it go?"

"Time for another stent."

I heard the intake of breath and waited. She would work through this news on her own. The day I was born, she'd faced a difficult decision: subject her newborn to a series of open heart surgeries over the next several years, hoping for a good outcome, or let her baby die. Before every surgery, she was given the same choice. It wasn't until I was seventeen and sat through the doctor's discussion of my options that I understood what she'd had to face. I'd thought my end of it was bad, but it paled in comparison to what my mom must have gone through.

Since then, advancements have gotten so great that they no longer needed to crack my chest open to make minor repairs. No longer was I dealing with ten to twelve week recovery periods. It would be a week of pain and very low energy. By the second week, I'd be limited in my activities but the pain would be replaced by soreness.

My mom would work through all this. I just had to give her time. "Oh, sweetie, like the last time?"

"Yeah, but he's using a different type of stent."

"Okay," she said, processing. She was thinking about all the time I'd spent in the hospital when I was a kid. All the nights she slept on a cot in my room, all the nurses she knew by name, all the other kids and moms who shared our floor. She'd remember all this and then send up a silent prayer of thanks that I was still living and a big plea to make this procedure go well. "When are we doing this?"

My heart sped up at her words. Not that I doubted it, but it felt good to know that my mom would be going with me like she had the last time and every time before. She'd been my rock when my dad couldn't come into the room without getting teary. The nurses said that always happened. The dads had a hard time dealing with seeing their kids so fragile. It was up to the moms to keep it together. No crying allowed on the pediatric ward. It was a rule among the kids.

"Couple weeks," I said.

"You'll stay with us."

"Thanks, Mom, but we'll see."

She'd take the next couple of weeks to try to convince me otherwise, but I couldn't always run to my mommy. I was an adult now, not a college student, not a junior in high school, and not a small kid. This would keep happening. At some point I'd have to learn to deal with it on my own.

Chapter 4

When I pulled into my driveway, I saw the back of a bundled figure on my doorstep. She turned at the sound of my car, and I recognized my new neighbor. My picnic basket hung from the bend of her arm. Her face showed a momentary flash of disappointment before a smile surfaced. I would have bet that she was hoping she could leave the picnic basket on my front porch without having to be neighborly.

She started toward me as I parked. It had been a long drive back from the city and my nerves were still fried from my doctor's appointment. I was eager to be home, not necessarily to host a guest, but happy for the company to keep from overanalyzing my health status.

"I wasn't sure if you were home." Her voice met me when I surfaced from the garage.

"I am now. Hello, Lena, nice to see you." *Even if you fooled me by using your middle name instead of the one I expected from your résumé.* Had I known I'd be living next door to the woman I helped hire, I might have been more insistent with my offer to help her unpack.

"Hi." Her face colored, embarrassed at having not started with that. "I don't want to keep you. I just wanted to return your picnic basket."

I smiled with welcome. "Good timing. I'm about to make coffee."

"I should be going." She extended the empty basket toward me.

I smiled wider and stepped around her, ignoring the proffered basket. "You like coffee; you told me. I bet your house is still in boxes. Come inside, have a cup with me."

She glared, but under her breath, I heard, "Bossy."

"I am, thanks. It's one of my best qualities." I flashed another grin on my way to the door. She had no choice but to follow.

Once inside, I shed my parka and boots then held my hands up for her jacket, hooking it on a peg. She looked down at her boots then at my hardwood floors past the mudroom. I pointed to the extra pair of slippers, stepping into mine. I left her to make the decision about getting comfortable, heading into the kitchen to start the coffeemaker right away. I'd be lucky if I kept her caged for the time it took to pour two cups.

"Are you settling in okay?" I called out, pulling down the mugs and setting them on the breakfast bar.

"I am," she said, not having grown any chattier since last week. She entered the kitchen and took a seat, placing her hands in her lap instead of resting elbows on the countertop. Either she was a graduate of a perfect posture class or trying hard not to make an impact on my space.

She was even more attractive than I remembered. Her hair was pinned back at the sides today, smooth and shiny, showing every beautiful angle of her face. This was her third hairstyle in the three times I'd seen her. I wondered how many more ways she could arrange that magnificent mane of hers. My whisper fine locks looked best left alone to brush against my shoulders, but I found myself experiencing hairstyle envy. Add her snug jeans and form fitting cashmere sweater and it was all I could do not to eat her alive with my eyes.

"Everything working okay in your house? Need any recommendations on repair people?"

Her eyebrows shot up. "Is there something you know that I should?"

"No," I rushed to assure her. "But it's been more than a year since the McGraths last came through. Lots of snow, below zero temps, unattended pipes and water heater, all sources of trouble."

A soft laugh came from her lips. It would have been a nice sound if the look on her face wasn't haughty. "Only an idiot buys a place without an inspection."

"Ah." I wasn't sure where to go from there. Busying myself with pouring the coffee, I searched for another topic. "Where are you from?"

Her look turned suspicious. "East coast."

How specific. Would I get a state out of her without running a background check? "I went to school in Philly. Loved it, but missed this place, so I moved back after a couple years in the workforce."

"It is lovely here." Her gaze went to the sliders leading to my backyard, which doubled as a plush forest. At least we could agree on that.

"Are you a skier?"

"Yes, you?"

"Why else live here?"

"Exactly," she agreed.

"Independently wealthy or do you plan to get a job here?" I meant it as a joke, but the shocked then almost angry expression that flashed across her face forced the levity from me.

She managed to will calm into her expression. "I've got a job."

I knew that but wasn't about to chance her thinking I had been spying on her. "Wonderful."

"I think it is." Her genuine response validated my school board vote.

"Somewhere I might know?"

Her eyes lifted to mine, blinking twice. "I'm a principal."

"Oh, right, at the high school." I debated whether I should tell her I'd been one of the reasons she got hired. No, probably not a good idea. "I thought I recognized you out front when I dropped off my neighbor the other day."

"You drive your neighbor to school?"

"Rarely, but she was running late."

"I didn't realize the Cranes or the mayor had high school age children."

I should have guessed that Spence and the Cranes had already introduced themselves. Nancy and Calvin probably showed up before the movers even got out of the truck. Nancy considered herself the neighborhood watch captain. A neighborhood of four whole houses. Tough beat.

"They don't. This neighbor lives by my office building. She shovels our driveway and mows the lawn in the summer. Good kid, best athlete you've got."

"Ashlyn," she said after going through a mental list of kids at her school. After only a week, she already knew many if not all of the kids? Impressive, and further validation for my vote.

"She's a great kid. If you need your yard taken care of in the summer, she's the one you want to go to."

Lena chuckled, fondness spilling with the sound. "Thanks for the tip." She took another sip of coffee and set her cup down with finality. "I should get going. I appreciate the coffee and the welcome basket. Very tasty."

"Where did I land on the thirty-five point scale?"

"Well," she drew out, getting up from the stool. Her movement was fluid like a bubble rising in a lava lamp. "I've only had the two samples. Can't make a judgment based on two items." Before heading to the front door, she flashed a wicked smile, sparking a raw tingle in my stomach. With her provocative challenge, she'd just managed to coerce more baked goods from me.

I had to applaud her. Not many people could make me reconsider my initial reaction to having a new full-time neighbor.

From the Journal of Lena Coleridge:

Made it through my first week at school. It still feels strange being someplace new. The staff is leery and the kids aren't used to me yet, but I expected that. My vice principal, Kirsten, seems to want me to succeed. What a change of pace that is. Paul the Prick would have sabotaged every move had he been my vice principal here. God, I'm glad I left Baltimore.

Took advantage of our half day today and finally got up on the mountain. It felt good. I still can't believe it's so close now. I should have moved here years ago. Who knew that being able to come home from work and practically ski out from my backyard would bring such calm? I'll have to test one of the cross country tracks tomorrow. Snow as psychotherapy. I wouldn't have believed it before moving here.

All it took was a couple hours of skiing and I was ready to face my neighbor again. I almost lucked out, but she drove up just as I was leaving her picnic basket. No hat hair tonight, and my, she looked good. Young, but good. Just the body type I like, slender and petite with proportionate curves. Those eyes of hers, translucent peacock blue, simply mesmerizing. From what I've seen, her attitude is easy going with a touch of snide. The perfect antidote for my temper. She would be trouble if she weren't so young, straight, and involved.

That's one thing about this place. You learn really quickly who is with whom. Three teachers practically fell over themselves telling me about my two neighbors, Glory and Spencer. I never would have put them together, but whatever works.

Super sweet, that lady. Made me coffee, didn't pry too much, seemed happy to know I was settling in at home and work. Maybe it's the whole thing with Regina that has me predisposed to be cautious around Glory. I'm over that gold digging user. Way over her. So why am I letting the actions of another young, beautiful woman affect how I feel about this one? If I want more of her fabulous coffee, delicious zucchini bread, and agreeable companionship, I'm going to have to drop that false association.

Chapter 5

The sound of a car pulling into my driveway was unexpected. My best friend slash business partner coming through my front door without knocking wasn't. We treated our homes like we lived in both and had been since becoming friends in high school as the two newest transplants. It wasn't easy trying to break into the long formed groups at school. For an international student like Mei, it was next to impossible. Our new kid status put us together, and we've never looked back.

"Hey, Glor, how'd your week go?" Mei reached up and pulled her stick straight black hair into a twist knot as she advanced toward me. The extra pink in her cheeks told me she'd left work early to go skiing today. The color looked good on her round, makeup-free face. So did her button nose and cute chin.

I grabbed the coffeepot to refill. I knew why she was here, she knew why she was here, and it had nothing to do with a casual howdy. When I turned back, she was re-twisting her knot, tipping her anxiety.

She let a few more seconds of silence pass before slapping her hand down on my countertop. "Come on, how'd it go? You're okay, right? Clean bill of health?" Her caramel brown eyes, unusual for her Chinese heritage, always displayed every emotion she endured.

She'd been the only friend to come visit me in the hospital during my junior year, one of only two friends to stop by my house during my recovery, and the only friend to treat me the exact same way as she had prior to and after my surgery. If I hadn't been convinced how good a friend she was before, I would have killed for her afterward.

"Trouble with a stent," I told her.

"Like the deal in college?"

"Yep, possibly more work this time."

She came around the island and pulled me into her. She liked hugging, always had, but this hug was for me not her, and I appreciated it all the more. "When?"

"Two weeks."

"Want me to move in?"

We both laughed. We already spent eight to twelve hours a day together at work. "You're here enough, lady."

"True," she drew out the word, testing to see if I wanted to say any more.

One look told her I wasn't ready yet. She hopped up onto the countertop, settling her skinny behind on the hard surface. It was okay with her that I didn't want to talk, but she wasn't going anywhere. I handed her the coffee mug and leaned against the counter next to her dangling legs.

After taking a sip, she offered a topic she knew I'd bite on. "Spence thinks it's time to take the next step."

Many different thoughts and words of advice came to mind, but I'd given my opinions before. Rewording everything now wouldn't do either of us any good. "And Andy?"

Her head tucked against her chest in a moment of guilt. "He's running for re-election soon."

I rolled my eyes. I couldn't help it. "He's always running for re-election. He's never going to lose, not when he's the best judge we've got."

"He might if the town knew about his wife's affair." Her eyes dropped again. That word, technically correct, but so inapplicable for her situation. Her marriage hadn't been a marriage for many years.

"The town won't know. He doesn't know. You're going to decide what life you want to live, Mei. And once you do, stick to it, go through all the hard steps, and live that life."

She thought about that. Her head nodded in time to the thoughts going through her mind. "What if life with Andy is what I choose?"

Stay with the man who gives her no regard or be with the man who makes her heart giddy? Didn't sound like a tough choice to me, but I wasn't the one making the move. "Andy chose that in college. High school, actually. The town chose that life, your parents chose that life, you didn't really choose it. You have a choice now. Make the right one."

"You make it sound so easy."

"It starts with five simple words." *Andy, I want a divorce*, I thought. Words I hoped Mei would be brave enough to utter. After seven years of a lackluster marriage and many months in an affair that made her happier than I'd ever seen, I wasn't sure she'd go through with the request.

"I should do it, shouldn't I?"

"You should."

We'd had this conversation before. Mei's problem was that she couldn't break her husband's heart and disappoint the people who cared about her. What she didn't seem to get was that his heart cared more about his perception in town. They'd been together so long and had gotten married so young they didn't really have a marriage so much as a role. The perfect high school sweethearts.

As a respected judge, Andy wouldn't want to give that up. It didn't matter that he didn't have any passion for his wife. He was more concerned about their status in town. It could be a long hard fight, but Mei had to start it. Spencer was the love of her life. It was just too bad that she didn't know that until it was too late.

* * *

"Really? You're going to drop this on me now? A week before doomsday?" I stared at my least favorite client.

"You're a magician with this stuff, Glor. I didn't realize I'd hired and fired two other people. What's the big deal?"

"Only about four other state forms and twelve lines on your federal form which I've already finished. You were done, Keith, done. I was wrapping up my others."

"Jeez, sooorrry, but I do pay you, you know."

I knew. I didn't like it, but I knew. It meant that I'd have to do these fixes. If he weren't also my most billable client, I'd file an extension and encourage him elsewhere. "You know the rules. Any changes within a week of the fifteenth and it's triple the rate."

"That's a crime!" His outrage was comical. He did this every year, which was how I'd afforded the down payment on the construction loan for my house a few years ago.

"Take your forms someplace else, then." The reply slipped right out of my mouth. Maybe I did really want him to leave. Or maybe it was the fact that very soon I'd be heading in for my procedure, and I didn't want to waste my time on someone stupid like this idiot anymore.

"Bad mood, huh? Is this week getting to you, Glor? Ready to pack it in?"

I wanted to smack him, just for fun, just to see how he'd react. Instead I simply smiled and told him to get the hell out of my office. Grouchy, he could put up with, fired, he could not. The pink slip of paper reminding me of my medical appointment two days after the tax deadline had been picking at me all day. I was getting grouchy, something I didn't often feel. I really just wanted to get it over with. Not that having it over with would make me want to keep Keith as a client.

"That dude makes me want to bathe," Brooke pronounced as she walked into my office. "Why the hell isn't that weasel Ted trying to pick him off like so many of our other clients?"

I watched her plop her long frame into the chair Keith had just vacated. When one of us got a client, more than likely, we all got a client. Keith utilized our services far more than any of us wanted. As much as I resented Ted, the resident financial planner slash investment counselor slash tax advisor slash business attorney, and his smarmy ways of hitting on our clients, I had to commend him for staying away from a troublesome client like Keith. I doubted we'd ever lose the guy unless he decided to move to another town.

"Did you kick him?" she asked with a mischievous grin. It was Brooke's greatest fantasy to kick some of our clients in the shins. She liked to resort to her third grade tendencies when clients acted up. She felt if they were acting like children, she should be able to.

"I'll leave that pleasure for you."

"Speaking of pleasure, help me ditch my husband tonight. Come out and have some fun."

"A week before tax day? Are you high?"

She laughed, almost giggling, a sign that she'd been looking at her computer screens too long today and needed a break. "Every year you become a tax form zombie. Won't you have a minute to spare?"

"A minute, yes, the entire evening, no possible way."

"You're no fun."

"That's what I've been trying to tell you for years, Brooke. Time for you to figure out a way to ditch your husband for the night without using me as an excuse."

"But he likes when I go out with you."

"He likes having you out of the house. He doesn't really care with whom." After seventeen years of marriage, Brooke's husband appreciated some time alone, probably more than Brooke did.

"We could ask your new neighbor out with us. I haven't had the chance to meet her yet, but Izzy seems impressed." Brooke's daughter was a sophomore and, like many teenage girls, loved to talk.

"If I could go out, that would be a good idea. I'm sure she'd appreciate making new friends." I wasn't, but I didn't want to make her sound unfriendly.

"What's a good idea?" Mei stepped into the open doorway.

"Inviting Glory's new neighbor out with us tonight."

"Are we going out tonight?" She looked excited by the prospect and my heart fell. I hated disappointing her.

"If you convince Glory."

"Hazel could," Mei threatened.

"No she couldn't," Hazel called out, overhearing us. "Not when Glory's still got twenty plus clients to finish. But it would be nice to meet the newcomer."

"What's the 'sip on her?" Brooke looked back at Hazel.

"Not much. She's from Baltimore where she left as principal of a much larger high school."

My eyebrows shot up. Hazel shouldn't know that unless she'd asked Lena, but I couldn't see Lena being more forthcoming with her than she'd been with me. "Which board member told you that?"

"Well, I never." Hazel brought a hand to her chest and sucked in a gasp.

We laughed at her acting ability. "Terry?" I guessed about my fellow board member.

"Who else," she countered. "That man couldn't keep a secret if his life depended on it."

"What more do you know?" Brooke asked me.

"She likes baked items and coffee."

"That's it?" Brooke insisted.

"That's all you'll get from me. Go introduce yourself. You've got a kid in high school, the perfect excuse."

"Might have to do that, or you could just invite her out tonight."

We laughed again at Brooke's determination. It was a tempting offer, but with my deadline, I couldn't afford to entertain the thought. No matter how much I'd like to see Lena try to deflect Brooke and Hazel's attempts to squeeze information from her.

Chapter 6

Rhythmic beeping and the acrid smell of antiseptic hastened my awakening. Mom's face hovered over me, smiling, but worried. My chest hurt but not nearly as much as my neck and leg. It took half a minute before I could hear Mom's voice, another half minute before I understood her words.

"How do you feel?"

"I," I started but my mouth was so dry I couldn't talk. I tried clearing my throat but felt it in everything that hurt.

A straw and cup appeared where Mom's face was. I swigged in some cool water and felt the liquid travel all the way down to my empty stomach.

"Better?"

"Thanks."

Fogginess surrounded my thoughts. I looked past my mom out the window to a view that I didn't recognize. I turned my head and felt a sharp pain in my neck but not before I spotted someone sleeping in a hospital bed a few feet away. That's right. I was in the hospital. These drugs always did a number on me. Not enough to take away all the pain, but they made me sleepy enough to ignore it.

"Doc Pickford said everything went great."

"Everything?" I knew the answer despite my foggy brain.

"He couldn't in get through the femoral."

"No kidding." I reached up to my neck but the motion made me wince. It really hurt. I felt for the bandage and wondered if I looked like a true vampire victim now. If it took more than two stitches to close, I'd have to start applying concealer every day until the scar faded.

"He got in the stent. That's all that matters, honey."

"I know, Mom."

"Do you feel okay?"

"My neck feels like I got shivved. My leg, too. Did they do the operation in a prison yard?"

She shook her head and tried not to smile. Relief passed over her face. If I was making jokes, she knew I was okay.

"When can I leave?"

"Tomorrow, and don't even try it, young lady. You're staying as long as the doc says you're going to stay."

"She's up?" Gail, the night duty nurse, walked into the room.

"And complaining," the traitor formerly known as my mother told her.

"Hey, Gail. Can the doctor sign me out now?"

"Aren't you hilarious?" she said, checking my IV and monitors. "Even if he didn't specifically tell me that you're not going anywhere until tomorrow morning, do you really think I could find a doctor in a hospital at this hour? Lie back and deal."

They both ignored the disgruntled sound I made. Staying the night was never fun. They always insisted on morning sponge baths even if you could do it yourself and you were leaving that day anyway. Plus the food sucked and the nurses kept waking you every two hours to make sure you're still alive.

Yeah, Mom called it. I was complaining. I had woken up and should be focusing on that achievement. I was in store for another few weeks of aches and slow motion movement. After that, I should feel like a teenager with all the energy I'd gain. I could deal with a night in the hospital.

By the next morning, it felt like I'd been there a week. Hospitals always did that to me. I signed the release papers without even reading them and went through a morning workout just loading into the car. The drive would take a few hours, but I didn't care. Happiness was the sight of a hospital in my rearview mirror.

"Wake up, honey," Mom said.

My eyes opened to the unbelievable sight of my garage door. I didn't remember falling asleep, but Mom was already walking around to my side of the car. The door to my house opened and Dad, Spence, and Mei spilled out onto the porch. I moved to open the car door and flinched. Something felt like it tore open in my neck.

"You okay, hon?" Mom opened the door for me.

"Yep, just forgot to move slowly." Like an idiot.

Gravity helped slide me out of the car and I managed to stand without much fuss. Walking was another matter. My leg had stiffened up on the drive, making me regret asking the doctor to try using my femoral artery before the carotid. Even a failed attempt meant a hole, stitches, and pain in my groin. I'd be walking with a limp for more than a week and he still had to force the stent in through my neck anyway.

To avoid stabbing pain with each step, I shuffle walked like a prisoner in ankle cuffs for the first time. The path to my house seemed to stretch to impossible lengths before my eyes. All the snow and ice didn't help matters much. Dad and Spence trotted over to help, seizing my arms and practically lifting me along the path. I bit down on the screech of pain because it was the only way I'd get into the house. My strength wouldn't have lasted past the garage door.

"I wish you'd stay with us," Mom repeated as they maneuvered me onto the sofa.

"My house doesn't have stairs, Mom." Good thing, too. We'd just found out that I couldn't lift my leg up a full riser without suffering a knife wound to my groin.

"You're staying here anyway, Dana," Dad told her.

"Slumber party," Mei announced, pointing at her bag near the hallway to the bedrooms.

"I can manage, guys."

They both rolled their eyes. Even if I weren't lying, they weren't going to leave me alone. I knew I'd be okay to get to the bathroom and the kitchen but staying long enough to make dinner would be difficult. Having Mom and Mei here would be like living with a house staff.

"How bad is it?" Spence asked, adjusting a pillow to prop me up. He'd been the other person besides Mei to come visit me after my surgery in high school. Most people were freaked out by sickness, teenagers especially. Not Spencer. He showed up after baseball practice, only missing days when he had games. He became one of my best friends that month.

"Not too bad now that I'm home." Tomorrow it would really start hurting once the pain meds were out of my system, but I'd manage it with ibuprofen.

"Good. I'll get out of your hair for today." He kissed my cheek.

"Go do mayorly things, and take my dad with you," I pleaded. Having Dad here made us all nervous. He'd be much better when I could walk without looking like I was marching on broken glass with every step.

"Sure thing." He grabbed my dad's arm. "We're out of here, Henry. Let the ladies have their fun."

"You sure, honey?" Dad looked hopeful that I was well enough to dismiss them.

"We're sure," Mom answered for me. "You guys take off."

Mei shuttled them to the door as Mom fussed over me on the couch. She'd be like this for the next couple days until the throbbing pain passed on to aches. I'd get to sore by next week. By three, all traces of soreness would be gone, and I'd be all set for hopefully years—decades if I could manage it.

I gazed at my mom and best friend, realizing how lucky I was to have them. Some mothers might have checked out with a sick child to block the heartache. Most best friends would have decided that they had better things to do than sit by a bedside. Not these two. I felt as lucky to have them as I did to be born in a year when my condition was no longer an automatic death warrant.

"Hungry?" Mom asked, heading to the kitchen. She didn't fool me. She already had my favorite all ready to warm up.

Mei winked at me, pulling up my legs to push a pillow under my knees. She knew my mom was shoving something into the oven whether I was hungry or not.

I laughed then clutched my neck and chest. That really hurt. I always forgot that. Coughing and sneezing were the worst, like the lash of a whip followed by molten steel rolling down my neck and chest. Good times, but I could manage for a couple of weeks. It would all be worth it once the pain was gone.

Chapter 7

Freedom never felt so good. My mother had only agreed to go back home because my friends would be taking shifts for meals and visits over the next few days. That would continue until I was walking without a limp and able to turn my neck without the bonus dull throbbing. At least my chest had stopped hurting and I was one week closer to being whole again.

I stepped out onto my porch and let the fresh air revitalize me. Crisp still, but not frigid. The snow was melting and would soon be gone. My dad had cleared my driveway for probably the last time this season while I was recuperating. I felt good enough to shovel it now, not that I'd be able to do it. Just walking the length of my wraparound porch sucked all of my energy, but I felt good enough to try.

One of the willow chairs on my porch beckoned. I eased into the chair and settled in. I could watch the forest around me for hours. It was my own reality television series. In the winter there wasn't much to look at, but I still liked the way the snow weighed down the limbs of the pine trees and clung to the spindly trunks of the aspen trees.

The sound of huffing had me rotating stiffly to check out my driveway. A blur of white came bounding toward me. Only the black nose and black tipped ear were clearly visible among the snow. Someone called out as the dog reached my steps and headed straight for me.

He plowed his snout right into my lap, tail wagging eagerly. No fear of people for this dog.

"Hello, pup." I set my coffee down and reached for his ears, rubbing vigorously. "Haven't seen you before."

"Kitty!"

I looked up to find my neighbor standing at the foot of my driveway, hip jutted, foot tapping, another smaller dog relaxing at her side. "Kitty?"

Lena shrugged and moved forward when she saw her dog wasn't going to back away from my massaging hands. "It's to prompt me to think of a real name."

"Is he new?" I re-examined the dog. He had to be two or three years old.

"Just got him last week at the shelter. I went in for this one here." She pointed down at what looked like a schnauzer next to her.

"And came away with two?"

"They were best buds. What was I supposed to do?"

I grinned. We both knew she'd been suckered, but I liked that she didn't seem to mind. I inclined my head at the chair next to me. She hesitated but didn't have much choice when the bonus dog didn't move. The small grey dog settled between us. "Looks like you got two of the best. I recognize that one as a schnauzer, but what have we got here?"

"Pit bull mix." Her chin lifted, almost like she was waiting for me to object. After thirty seconds of silence, it dropped and she looked away. "My co-op would never have allowed a pit bull where I used to live."

"You won't find that a problem here." I shifted to Kitty's hind quarters and started scratching. His head dipped and he went into bliss.

"I can see that." She stroked the curly chin of the smaller dog.

"You should probably nix the name. What about that one?"

"Fender." The schnauzer wiggled his behind at the sound of his name.

"Nice."

"Thanks." She glanced around. "You have a great view here."

"Almost exactly like yours, but from the other side." I got her to smile. "Want some coffee?"

"We won't stay long."

"Half a cup?" I wouldn't give her an out, already pouring from the thermos I'd brought out with me. It was so nice to talk to someone who didn't ask how I was feeling or look at me like I might break in half with every move I made.

"You should open a coffee shop." She accepted the mug and warmed both hands while sniffing the aroma.

"That good, huh?"

"I held on to your thermos for an extra day just for the lingering scent."

I laughed. She was loosening up. Bound in a parka and jeans, she looked like a real local. Only the fact that she'd swept her hair up into a messy knot leaving her ears exposed gave away her status as new to the area. She'd misjudged how cold it was before she started walking tonight. Her nose would soon become just as red as her ears.

"You had a steady stream of people in and out of your place this past week. Are you running a side business I should know about?"

My smile faltered, but then I realized that she didn't know about me. It seemed like everyone else in town did, but this woman thought I was as robust and healthy as anyone else. "Book club."

She laughed, the sound hearty and warm. "Every day?"

"I like to read."

Her hands came off Fender, waving in surrender. "I just bet."

"You wanted to join?"

"Every day for a week? I couldn't possibly keep up with that schedule. What are you guys reading, complete trash?"

"Nothing wrong with mindless lit."

She stared at me, not one ounce of humor on her face. "If you say so." Deadpan worked for her.

Her eyes drifted down to the edge of my turtleneck. I reached up and checked that my collar covered the bandage that would come off with the stitches tomorrow. Nothing appeared out of order, but I hitched up the shirt just in case. She watched my fingers make the adjustment, scrutinizing like she was trying to find Waldo.

I rushed to deflect her attention. "You'd join for my coffee."

"That's true." She tipped the last of the coffee into her mouth.

"I've got more."

"I'll remember that." She stood up and slapped her thigh. Kitty looked over and realized he was going to have to leave. He backed into me for one last rub then bounded off the porch to join Fender on their walk back. "Glad it wasn't something else."

I steeled my expression, searching hers. It was possible that she'd run into someone who spilled the story about my procedure. I would hope that they'd keep my medical condition private from someone I hardly knew. It was too much to ask that they wouldn't tell her other things about me, but my medical history should be off the table.

"Stop by anytime."

She waved and headed out. Our third meeting and I already felt like she was becoming a friend.

From the Journal of Lena Coleridge:

Good day today. The kids seemed to respond to the assembly. I worried for nothing again. Kids need rules and guidelines. Some might drag their heels, but they're all mostly good. None of these kids strike me as violent, a nice change from Baltimore. Hormone induced stupidity for sure, but for the most part, they have good intentions.

Kirsten is becoming a trusted ally. She's not resentful at all—big relief. Thought I'd get some attitude when she lost her gig as interim principal, but she prefers being a vice principal. Ugh, so not for me. She's great for bouncing ideas around and a good conversationalist in general. Focuses on work a little too much, but I can't be choosey with friends in a small town. Another downside I'm learning to live with.

Rounding out the good day, I stopped over at Glory's. Nothing to worry about there. Turns out all those people coming and going from her house this past week wasn't because of bad news. Thought it might have been a death in the family, but she joked about a book club. I'm curious, but she didn't seem sad, a little tired but not sad, and I don't know her well enough to force the issue. Maybe it was a town project or something. People keep telling me there are all sorts of festivals that happen in the off season. She could be on the town council for all I know. She certainly has the likable personality for it. I should trust Kitty—and change his name—but for now, trust him. He's a good judge of character. Perhaps we'll be stopping by on our evening walks more often. Her coffee and various baked items aren't the only attractive things about her.

Chapter 8

The smell of must still lingered in the school district boardroom, despite the recent renovation. I'd recommended a full reno during the last budget meeting not just the cosmetic changes that were made. Three meetings later, the rest of the board now agreed with me. It was one of two topics we had slated for what should have been a short last meeting of the school year. When I'd arrived, I was shocked to see all the seats full. Either this town was starved for entertainment or they felt there was something other than drywall bids and next year's meeting dates to discuss tonight.

"Glor," Terry, the superintendent of the district, greeted as I took my place on the dais two seats over from him. "How are you feeling?"

Three weeks had passed. I felt great, but that didn't stop everyone in town who hadn't yet checked in from asking after my health. Small towns sucked sometimes. Big city life with no one knowing about my heart condition and when I'd had surgery sure had great appeal at times.

"Fine, thanks, Terry. Big crowd tonight, huh?" I wanted to get his mind back on the matter at hand. Enough concern already. Time for something else big to happen and take me off the gossip list.

"Huge. A lot of people signed up for public comments." He glanced over at the door where people were signing in. He wasn't concerned about what they'd say. He was concerned he'd miss tonight's episode of

Dancing with the Stars. We'd spent many pre-meeting sessions rehashing what happened on the show. Even if I liked the show, I wouldn't have to watch it with his exhaustive reports.

We were soon joined by the other three members of the board, and Terry rapped his gavel to start the meeting. He called roll, which I'd never understood since everyone could see us sitting behind our name plates and everyone in the audience knew who we were, but he liked to stick with tradition.

When I acknowledged my presence I caught movement in the second row on the aisle. Lena's face swung up and over to stare at me, an astonished smile on her face.

"Hello, neighbor. Surprised?" I could tell by the degree of astonishment that she hadn't looked closely at the names on her offer letter.

Once we'd gone through the boring business that could just as easily have been written up in a newsletter and distributed, Terry opened the floor for comments. His assistant called out from her list, prompting the first public comment in a year since we'd voted down upgrading the uniforms for the boys' basketball team. Voted down because they weren't going to upgrade the girls' uniforms at the same time. Some people in town felt that since the boys' team did much better than the girls' that they should have new uniforms. Surprisingly, three of the board members initially agreed.

One of my clients, Rebecca, scurried down the aisle from the back and tapped the microphone. This was the first time I'd ever seen her in a meeting much less attempt to speak out. Her son, Jaden, wasn't exactly a stellar student or athlete. In fact, I think he pretty much only excelled at lunch.

"Are you aware that there's been a policy change regarding suspensions at the high school? Apparently the *new* principal doesn't understand how we do things around here and has taken it upon *herself* to institute new policies and procedures." She stressed certain words as if we weren't all aware that we had a new principal who was female.

Terry swiveled his head to look at us, obviously wondering if any of us knew there'd been a policy change. I hadn't heard about it, but many of the parents made agreement noises, clearly having signed up to talk about the same thing.

"We're all very concerned about how this will affect our children," Rebecca continued.

Heads nodded throughout the room, and I had to turn away to hide my smile. Who knew this many parents had kids who have been or were in danger of being suspended? It always seemed like the parents with kids who acted up had the loudest voices. Perhaps that was why their kids acted up. They learned it from their parents.

"This woman you hired," she began, giving each of us a steely glare for having the nerve to hire someone to fill an important position, "has decided to enforce unnecessarily strict rules. Our students are suffering the punishment, and these minor discretions are being recorded on their permanent records. It's hard enough for kids to get into college these days. Having a suspension on their record could ruin their chances."

Knowing her nightmare of son, Jaden, I wanted to laugh out loud. He was the kind of kid who deserved to spend time in a military school. I sought out Lena whose eyes were trained on Rebecca, looking calm but clearly ready to speak if she needed to.

"What policies are you talking about?" Terry finally asked.

"She's suspending kids for being tardy and for speaking out in class. She's even suspending kids for pranks they play on each other."

Terry glanced at me as if I'd take over. I was the member with the most objectivity when it came to policy issues. Since I didn't have a kid that could be caught up in these rules, they often looked to me to comment.

I looked again at Lena before addressing Rebecca. "I take it Jaden has been suspended?"

A low chuckle went through the crowd before some of them realized that their kids were in the same pool. Rebecca often acted like she starred in her own version of *Real Housewives* of Aspen. Dramatic wouldn't do her personality justice. Mess with her son and you'd find your car scratched by one of her many diamond rings.

"Not only has he been suspended, Glory, but it's going on his record. He's been forced to sit in a prison cell for five days."

"What?" Mitch, the owner of a car dealership in town, leaned onto his forearms, showing interest for the first time in many months.

"She's putting them into closets at school and making them sit there all day with nothing to do."

Four other mothers agreed audibly as Terry decided what to do. He leaned in to whisper to Jennifer, a bank manager in town. She shook her head and leaned over to whisper to me. "Suggestions?" she asked, clearly passing on Terry's confusion.

"Ms. Coleridge? Would you like to come up and go through the changes you've implemented?" I hoped my tone didn't sound accusatory. She should know she had the authority to institute any policy she wanted.

Lena stared at me for a moment before nodding and rising from her seat. She headed over to the microphone, but Terry waved her up to sit at the extra chair beside me. He introduced her to the crowd for those people who somehow didn't know we had a new principal and resident of the town.

"Why don't you start with what makes a student eligible for suspension rather than detention?" Terry began.

Lena faced the crowd when she spoke. "Thank you for the opportunity to address everyone's concerns. As the board members know, during my interview you brought up issues surrounding the carefree disregard of rules by the young men and women in our school. I spent a few weeks observing this very concern before deciding to institute measurable rules. I held an assembly to explain the new rules and consequences. Every student attended and had to sign an acknowledgement stating that they understood and would abide by the rules."

Sounded fair to me, but the eruption of noise from the crowd told me I was in the minority on this view. Shouts of "they're just kids," or "you can't hold them to adult standards," and "give them a break," came out. I felt Lena go rigid next to me. I wanted to reach out and squeeze her arm in support, but I didn't know her that well and she might not be a touchy, feely type.

"These are not just kids," Lena told them. "They're young adults. They understand consequences and have the capacity to deal with them."

Go, neighbor! I was digging this feisty lady.

"Thanks to you, Jaden has had one college offer rescinded."

"What?" Mitch repeated, effectively doubling the comments he's made in one year.

"His suspension went on his record. USC received the updated information and reduced him to the waiting list."

That moron got into USC? Perhaps daddy's money had something to do with it. More importantly, though, had none of his other suspensions gone on his record? What kind of a disciplinary system was that?

"Suspensions are always recorded." Lena's voice was cool. It was good to see she could be more clipped with other people. In fact, she seemed downright warm to me now that I was seeing her in an adversarial position.

"William never put them on record. The worst he'd do is send the boy home for the rest of the day."

"That might explain why your son felt he could get away with some of the things he's been doing," Lena said after many people in the crowd voiced their support for our late principal's system.

"Don't you tell me that my son is a problem, lady. Right now, you're the only problem in this room."

"Rebecca," I spoke up and waited for her fiery eyes to shift to me. Her status as my client and my recent health scare made the glare soften a bit. "As the principal, Ms. Coleridge is able to set and enforce rules. As long as she doesn't discriminate in the enforcement of these rules, she's within her duties as principal."

"You wouldn't be saying that if your kid was the one getting blackballed by colleges," she retorted before her hand came up to cover her mouth. Sorrow entered her expression. She obviously realized that with my condition, I might not be able to have kids. What she didn't know was that I'd never wanted them.

Terry tried to step in and smooth things over. "I'm sure this is something that can have a different outcome, right, Lena?"

My head whipped around to stare at him. Had he really just suggested that? Terry could crumple in a light summer breeze.

"The student in question violated not one, but three rules," Lena told him. "He deserved his suspension. In fact, I could have made a case for expulsion."

"That's complete bull!" Rebecca yelled.

Lena waited for the audience to settle after the outburst. "Your son stripped off a boy's towel after gym class then shoved him naked into the girl's locker room, barring his escape while calling him a 'queer' over and over. Your son is a bully at best and should be very happy that the victim didn't want to press charges or have him expelled. He humiliated that boy in front of a locker room full of girls. They were also prevented from leaving until the taunting grew loud enough to be heard by the girls' P.E. teacher from her office. Be grateful I didn't insist on expulsion."

My mouth had nudged from ajar to wide open. That poor boy and those poor girls must have been so uncomfortable. Jaden had rocketed past being a mild pain in the ass to a sociopath in my opinion. Lena was right. He's damn lucky he didn't get expelled or even jailed for his actions.

The crowd had grown quiet upon learning what had gotten Rebecca's son in trouble. New admiration for Lena seemed to grow from the others, especially the board.

"You're exaggerating. Boys play pranks. My son wouldn't hurt anyone. He certainly doesn't belong in your storage closet prison cell."

"Rebecca," Jennifer started, clearly shocked by what Lena had said. "I'm sure that Jaden didn't think it all the way through, but I have to agree with Ms. Coleridge's assessment and punishment. If something like that had happened to my daughter, I don't think I'd stop the sheriff from arresting him."

"He'd never do something like that to a girl, of course. My son is a good boy. He and his friends were having a little fun at the expense of another boy. That's just high school. Everyone feels picked on."

"My job as a principal is to make sure that everyone is treated equally and with the respect that every person deserves," Lena said with confidence. "I clearly communicated that I wouldn't accept mistreatment of any kind. Every student understands the rules I've established and has signed off on them."

"How can you justify sticking a child in a closet for nine hours a day?" Rebecca shot back. Even though she'd lost some of the crowd with what her son had done, many of them looked to Lena for her response.

"It's seven hours in a vacant supply room. They have a chair and a desk with two breaks and lunch taken outside. Suspension shouldn't be a vacation from school where kids stay home and play video games all day. My suspensions are the high school version of a time out. They have nothing to do but think about what got them stuck in there. Believe me, very few kids end up suspended again after staying in my time outs."

No, ma'am. I wouldn't imagine any kid could stand to spend seven hours a day doing absolutely nothing.

"But it's not safe for them," Inez, mother of six sons, spoke up from her seat.

"We have cameras monitoring the rooms. My vice principal and I are just across the hall from them. The kids are well cared for. They're bored out of their minds, but they'll think twice before they decide to get into trouble again."

"It just seems so harsh," Lois, another of my clients, spoke up. "For being tardy? Can't you just put them in detention?"

Lena leaned forward and spoke in a softer tone. "I do. They get detention for three, again after the fourth and fifth. At that point, detention is no longer a deterrent, but suspension is. Since your daughter was placed in suspension for a day because of it, not one student has been late to class. The few students who interrupt their teachers by clowning around or talking back have been model students since spending a day in suspension. My policies work. Your kids just need time to adjust."

"Terry?" Rebecca pleaded.

He looked torn for a moment. "I guess we could call a vote, but it does seem as if your son deserved the punishment he got."

I started forward, completely flabbergasted by his suggestion. "We're not voting. That's not the role of the board. We've hired an extremely qualified person after an exhaustive search to make all the decisions she wants about her school."

"But," Terry began then realized he didn't really have an argument just a swell of displeasure from a crowd.

"No, Ms. Coleridge is doing the job we hired her to do." I glanced over at Lena and realized I hadn't gone far enough. "And for the record, I completely support her decision to place those students in suspension and believe the new method is far better than letting the kids have time off from school."

"Yes, yes, of course," Terry decided to agree. Or maybe he noticed that his favorite show was on in five minutes. He disbanded the meeting with a crack of his gavel.

A rush of people moved up to catch us before we could leave. Thankfully, no one seemed to want to chat with me. Perhaps they knew they couldn't change my mind.

"You're on the board." Lena turned to me with a raised brow. "Why didn't you tell me you knew who I was that first night?"

I smiled, leaning in so that no one else would hear. "I thought we'd hired someone named Beatrice. I expected a tightly wound, bun wearing, librarian type."

Her mouth quirked into a smile before her head shook and ruefulness leaked in. I would have questioned it had I not been distracted by how great she smelled. Fresh like springtime in a rose garden. I could almost feel her skin touching mine and had to fight not to fall completely against her.

"You weren't in the interviews."

"I was out of town."

She eyed me up and down, the gaze palpable on my skin. "You were the third vote."

My mouth popped open. She shouldn't have known that the vote was 3-2. That would only serve to make her feel inadequate that it wasn't a unanimous vote. Which of my idiot co-board members would want her to feel like that? It had to be Mitch or Joel, the two no votes. Although, looking at Terry or Jennifer, I could believe they'd want to make themselves look good in her eyes. I really needed to quit this board.

"I'm sorry someone felt it necessary to tell you that. You have our complete support."

Her eyes gained a faraway look. "I wonder if I do."

Before I could assure her again that the board stood behind its initial decision, she stood and walked out of the room. I wanted to follow, but my exit got delayed by two clients who were more concerned about their tax refunds than their kids' status in high school.

From the Journal of Lena Coleridge:

I cannot believe Glory didn't tell me she was on the school board and the reason I was hired. She was probably gloating the entire time we've talked, knowing she held my fate in her hands. Showing up tonight without telling me she was going to be there. We had coffee together last night. She had to know I'd be shocked. Why hadn't she said anything?

She did support me, though. That was a pleasant surprise. Most board members are reluctant to my changes at first. Glory jumped on the bandwagon right away. She seems so unassuming when we chat. Now I know she can be authoritative when she wants. Denial Mom even shut up when Glory spoke.

What's an accountant doing on a school board, especially when she doesn't have kids? Wait, maybe she does. Just because I've never seen kids at her house doesn't mean she isn't divorced with a co-parenting plan. She's got to be too young to have a kid in my school. Will she be that supportive when her kid, if she has one, reaches high school?

I was expecting a lecture from her after the meeting. I shouldn't have told everyone what that boy did. I could have made my point without embarrassing the boy's mother. I've got to get control of my temper and not let it dictate what I say. Denial Mom was baiting me, and I should have stuck to my script. Instead I made her son's actions public. That wasn't smart. Terry was probably rethinking his vote to hire me. I need to be more careful. It doesn't matter that Glory seems to have my back. I deal with people's kids. Support will only last until I do something to the wrong precious kid.

Chapter 9

White bounding energy came streaking up my driveway and onto my porch before I'd managed to set down my beer. His nose went right into my free hand for a big lick before turning around and waiting for his hiney rub. I placed the beer on the side table and turned my attention to the dog. Out of my periphery, I noticed Lena appear on the street past the cluster of trees edging my property.

I disguised my smirk with a full smile, happy that she was starting to make this a common stop on her dog walking route. The weather had turned warmer, snow gone from everything but the mountains. I'd be out on my porch every night soon, probably wondering if she'd stop by every day.

"Kitty wanted to say hi," she said by way of greeting.

I nodded at the other chair and grabbed another bottle of beer from the cooler I always brought out in case Spencer or Mei stopped by. Or maybe I just hoped she'd be the one to make an appearance. I was beginning to look forward to these short recaps of our days.

"Kitty needs a real name."

"Like what?" One eyebrow quirked as she reached for the beer.

"He's your dog."

"I'm partial to Kitty." Her tone held a teasing lilt.

"Kitty it is, then." Two could play at that game. "Any more students thrown in lockup?"

"Funny."

She took a sip of her beer, forcing my eyes to her neck. I imagined licking the long, enticing column, devoting hours to the rich supple skin. Wrong thought to have when sitting inches away from a woman who had no interest in the licking. I barely knew her and we were neighbors. I really shouldn't be having these thoughts. With a pinch of my thigh, I got my mind back where it belonged.

"How many of my parents are your clients?"

My head tilted back against the chair. She was asking a semi-personal question? Covering new ground tonight. Too bad I had to shut it down. "I keep that confidential."

She acknowledged that with a tip of her head. "I just wondered if that was why they backed off so quickly last week."

"They backed off because everyone knows Jaden is a troublemaker, but no one guessed he could be a sociopath. Is the other boy truly okay?"

"It's hard to say. High school boys, you know."

"Yeah." Even if he hadn't been completely humiliated, getting him to talk about his feelings probably wasn't going to happen.

"I thought I'd get lucky and not have these kinds of problems in a smaller town, but I guess teenagers are the same everywhere."

I turned and studied her, hoping she wasn't regretting her decision to move. "Something tells me that having clear and understandable boundaries in place may make them behave a little better."

"Intolerance is something they usually pick up at home."

Nodding, I couldn't really argue that point. We didn't have much diversity here. That tended to influence attitudes. When I first moved here, I'd been shocked to find out that many of my new classmates had never met anyone of a different race or religion before. The influx of tourists since then has helped widen horizons, but we were still fairly homogonous in appearance and unadventurous in when it comes to point of view.

"We're going for a hike on Saturday," Lena announced, changing the topic. "We need a guide."

I smiled and rubbed Kitty again. "Sounds fun."

"Baked goods will of course be required."

I laughed this time. "Any requests?"

"Whatever you can make."

Not a picky woman? I could get used to that. Hiking, not so much, but an hour with her away from everything would be worth it. "Time?"

"Better wait till the afternoon to give the sun a chance to heat things up a bit more."

"There's a nice trail just out back here." I pointed toward a gap between the trees. The hill beyond my property limits provided some nice vistas of town and Ajax.

"Oh," she said, disappointment pinching her brow. "I thought we'd try Snowmass or Buttermilk."

A mountain? I couldn't do a mountain. I was good for ten minute spurts on steep inclines, but I wouldn't make it very far. Damn if I'd tell her why, though. She was the only person I knew who didn't worry about my condition, didn't know about it, or feel like there was something wrong with me.

"The resort is still making snow. We better stick to the lowlands."

"This summer, then."

"Sure." I'd figure out a way to get out of it later. I didn't want anything to dampen my excitement at being alone together. I knew it was fruitless to get excited. Even if she was gay, and I doubted Ms. Private here would share something like that with me, she's still my neighbor. Neighbors had the ability to keep watch on you and your actions. It could become stalkerish really fast.

"See you Saturday."

It's a date. With my straight neighbor, but still a date. I hadn't been on one of those in a while.

* * *

Weather wise, the day was as close to spring as it would get with snow patches still in sight. All I needed was a zip fleece, t-shirt, and jeans to stay warm on the trail. I'd packed light, knowing my staying power, but it was filled with the lightweight baked goods that would dazzle my companion.

Lena had shown up at my door, two dogs in tow and a backpack that looked like it would carry all the clothes she'd need for a month-long backpacking trip through Eastern Europe. Excitement glittered in her brown eyes. At that moment I recognized her for the true outdoorswoman she was. She wore the look almost as well as she wore the multitude of creative hairstyles. Even today's simple ponytail looked flawless on her.

Up ahead, she walked at a brisk pace not bothered by the incline on the trail so far. It would have been difficult to keep up if I were in shape. With my condition, I would be lucky to keep her in sight once we hit the steeper parts.

"Look, raccoons." I stopped, pointing off to the side.

She halted about ten paces ahead and came back to look. I evened out my breathing to keep from panting. Aerobic exercise drained my energy. For someone with half a heart, walking was considered aerobic. Hiking was the equivalent of a fitness boot camp for me.

"Make sure your trash can lid is locked every night if you decide to keep it outside."

She looked from the raccoons playing in the trees back to me. "Good tip. Not something I'd have to worry about at my co-op."

"Bet you didn't have this view at your co-op either."

"I woke up to the spectacular sight of a brick wall every morning. If I looked out the corner of my window I could just make out a line of dumpsters in the alley."

"Stunning."

She laughed and looked surprised by it. Amazing sound. I liked it more than I wanted to admit. Not that I had time to dwell on that with her swiveling and starting into a trot on the trail. As sexy as her long legs were, I now wanted to hack them off at the knees.

I kept up the best I could. My breath came in pants by the time I stopped again to retie both of my shoes. Glancing over her shoulder, she spotted me stopped on the trail. She came back and waited with a surprising amount of patience. My progress was painstaking, but she didn't seem to mind.

After an hour I was ready to throw up a white flag. Or maybe just throw up. I couldn't keep her pace. In fact, I seriously doubted I could make it all the way back without a stretcher. This had been a stupid idea. I should have known better than to try to impress a beautiful woman by exercising with her.

"Ready for a snack break?" I called out as a last hope.

She twirled with an eager smile on her face. Seeing the fifty feet between us, the smile slackened in confusion. She seemed troubled that she'd outpaced me so far and hadn't noticed it. The confusion disappeared when she saw me pull off my backpack. Eagerness took over. "Baked snacks?"

"Of course."

I took a seat on the nearest log and pulled in discreet breaths through my nose, letting them out through my mouth. Digging through my backpack, I found the tinfoil wrapped ginger cake I'd baked this morning. Her body brushed against mine as she sat down. I stopped myself from shivering at the contact. Or at least I thought I had.

"Are you cold?" she asked, reaching for one of the proffered tinfoil packages.

"No."

"Your lips are blue." Her eyes stayed on my lips, shooting a surge of arousal through me. They dropped downward after a moment. "So are your fingertips."

Damn. That happened when I pushed myself too hard. I'd called for the break just in time. Any farther and I might have passed out.

"I guess I must be." I had to offer some excuse for the lack of oxygen in my bloodstream. It was less shocking than telling her if she didn't slow down, she might need to give me CPR. I was a firm believer that one should save CPR for the second or third date. Why rush emergency medical care? It's really something to build up to in any relationship.

She rummaged through her backpack. "I have gloves and a sweater."

"I'll be fine now that the wind isn't blowing in my face. You have us jogging out here."

She bumped against me with a laugh. "Don't tell me you're out of shape. You don't look it. How often do you work out?"

Walking from the car to my house was a workout for me. So technically, every day, but it wasn't what she was asking.

"You're probably young enough that you don't need to work out yet. Am I right?"

"Not that young. I'm thirty."

She frowned momentarily before pushing air through her lips audibly. "You're practically a baby."

At thirty? She couldn't be much older. Not that it would matter. Facing mortality so young gave me an ageless perspective.

"And you're not?" I knew from her résumé that she was older but not by how much.

"I've got ten years on you."

She didn't look it, not by any standards. Sexy, lean, and poised, sure, but not ten years older. She must have a hell of a skin care regimen.

"Will you need a walker to get back down the trail?"

"Hilarious." She crumpled up the tin foil and shoved it into her backpack. "You're the one that's out of shape."

"You wolfed that down." I changed the subject. "Rating?"

"I'll post them when I'm ready." She grinned and fluttered her eyebrows. Then just as suddenly, she popped off the log and started back toward the trail.

I resisted a groan and got up to follow. We were only a hundred yards from the first viewpoint. It was beautiful enough to convince her we didn't have to go on. Next time, I'd bow out of hiking. We could enjoy the outdoors on a four-wheeler or inner tubing down the river in the summer. That was exercise I could handle.

Chapter 10

Spencer's job had many necessary evils, fundraisers being one of them. Often I'd volunteer as his plus one to act as a buffer for the many residents who'd spend these evenings accosting him for things. I didn't usually mind, but tonight I kind of wished I was back on my porch, hoping for a drop by of my favorite new neighbor.

"You look great tonight," Spence said, his trimmed beard hiding part of his smile. He was an attractive man, much more so than he'd been in high school. He had the kind of face that needed growing into. Now that he'd filled out a bit, his square face suited him better.

I eyed his tan suit and dark blue shirt and tie. Very stylish, if I do say so myself. Mei and I found it on our last shopping trip for her style-challenged husband. It wasn't unusual for us to call Spencer to tell him we'd found something he might like. He did the same for us. I had a new snow blower courtesy of his last trip to Denver.

"You've said, seven or eight times," I responded with a smile.

He never took anyone for granted. It was one of his best traits. With his old fashioned charm, he could make anyone feel special. It was probably why he'd been voted in as the youngest mayor of the town and had held the position for three years already.

"I'm behind, then and people won't stop raving about this suit. Nice pick."

"Thanks."

"What's a nice pick?" Andy, Mei's husband, asked when they joined us. He was a schmooze hound, knowing full well that a fundraiser was a great place to garner votes. He hadn't aged as well as Spence, being a year older than us. That extra year looked like a difference of ten now. It helped with his occupation, but the receding hairline would probably disappear in another five years.

"His suit. We found it when Mei was out looking for yours."

He nodded as if it were the most important thing he could agree with all night. "These ladies love their shopping, huh?" He elbowed Spence, whose only choice was to agree. We weren't shoppers, but Andy never bothered to learn that. He was perfectly happy thinking his wife was shopping with me and crashing at my house for the night when really she was spending time with Spencer.

If I were judgey, I'd have a problem with their affair. Thankfully, I'm not. Mei had been in a blissful high school romance with Andy when Spence became my good friend and, thereby, a friend of hers. Nothing sparked between them at the time because Andy was already talking marriage as soon as they graduated. It was always on the tip of my tongue to encourage her to wait, but Mei had been raised with a sense of duty. Her parents approved of Andy, and he made her happy. They didn't see a reason to wait, and Mei didn't know why she needed to.

That all changed last fall when Andy was on one of his many work trips out of town. Mei came over to my place for a movie night with Spence and me. I don't exactly recall how, but sometime that night, they'd fallen in love. I'd watched it happen. I'd never seen anything like it before or since. Movies try to capture that on screen, but it will never be depicted as well as seeing it happen live. Like moving from a soundproof, sterile room to the raunchy, vibrant city streets, the experience can never be portrayed. It must be lived.

For me, it had been shocking and touching then heartbreaking because Mei was married and Spence was a public figure. They tried to fight it for a while, but the affair happened and has been going on ever since. My parents and I were the only ones who knew. They both needed someone to talk to and their own parents might not understand.

"I think I spotted that one first," Mei said about Spencer's suit.

Andy didn't even blink at his wife's admission that she'd chosen clothes for another man. He'd never expressed jealousy or concern. He just assumed that after marrying Mei she'd continue to fawn all over him like she was still in high school. He didn't seem to get or maybe he just didn't care that Mei had grown up and they'd been growing apart for more than five years.

"Nice pick," Spencer repeated his compliment to her. He kept his tone neutral. He felt the guilt as much as Mei, but he'd never been in love. He wasn't about to give it up because of a legal complication. I had to agree with him on this one, even if I'd never been in love either.

"Are they feeding us at this thing?" Andy whined. He liked to eat. After being a judge, eating was his next favorite thing.

"Finger food, we're trying to keep it low cost."

"And you expect us to fork over dough when you don't even feed us?"

I resisted rolling my eyes. Andy always tried too hard with humor. I'd let it roll off me ever since I'd met him. He'd been Mei's boyfriend, a permanent attachment to her on some days, so I had to get used to him. Even after college and law school, he hadn't matured a whole lot.

"The town needs a community center, Andy."

"Sometimes I forget you're the mayor, Spence. We've managed without one for years. Why now?"

Spencer shouldn't have to justify this, but he took his duties as mayor seriously. "Families and kids need a low cost option for entertainment and learning opportunities to bring the townspeople closer together. It feels like I have to wade through ten thousand tourists before I spot a local in the winter. The community center can help us all feel more connected."

"Like a cult?" Andy joked.

"Andy," Mei warned. She became easily exasperated by him these days.

"Better benefits," Spencer quipped back.

"How much are you going for tonight?"

"One point five."

"Expensive, but it pays to have a friend who knows how much her clients can cough up." Andy winked at me.

"Andy," Mei warned more harshly this time. She mouthed an apology to me, but I shook it off.

"You forget that I also know how much you can cough up," I said, and his grin faded.

Spencer snickered. "Anything you can give would be appreciated, Andy. There are some nice silent auction items or if you just want to drop a check with Brandy."

"You should have been in sales, Spence." Andy grabbed Spencer's hand in a bone grinding handshake.

"He'd be terrific at it." Mitch, my board colleague, overheard and joined us with his wife. "No reason you can't start now, Spence. I could use you on the lot."

We had a good laugh at the idea of Spencer trying to sell cars to all the people who voted for him. "When I need a new car, I'll join up for the day to get an employee discount."

"I might take you up on that." Mitch gave me a once over. "When are you finally going to make an honest woman out of Eiben here?"

Spence and I glanced at each other before I responded as I usually did, "We're just friends, Mitch. Always have been."

Mitch, like many residents, believed that Spencer and I were a couple. The rumors had started after we both moved back to town and took up hanging out together. It didn't seem to matter how much we denied it. In fact, that usually made people think we were trying to keep our relationship secret. My friends knew the real story, but I stopped making an effort with acquaintances and clients. That it now helped Spencer and Mei didn't hurt either.

"Hello," a familiar voice spoke from behind me.

I turned to see my neighbor looking gorgeous in a tasteful black dress. Kirsten, the vice principal, and Rod, the elementary school principal, stood on either side of her. "Hi, all."

"Glory, good to see you looking well." Rod brushed his mustache against my cheek in greeting. We'd become friends when he was dating my realtor friend, but now he was engaged to Kirsten. I didn't know her as well, but we'd always been friendly. They seemed like a good match, much more so than he'd been with Rachel.

While they were saying hello to everyone, I studied my neighbor. She looked at home here as she had as a principal and as she does sitting on my porch. Her hair was loose tonight, hanging free to the middle of her back. I scanned the dark strands trying to name the product she used to keep it so polished no matter the style she chose. She wore an expensive set of ruby earrings and a matching bracelet. Not the kind of accessories most principals could afford. Come to think of it, her house, twice as large and extravagant as mine, wasn't something a principal should be able to afford. She must have made some good investments in her former job. That or she'd robbed a bank.

"A community center would be a wonderful stop for some of our kids, don't you think?" Lena asked her companions.

"If there's tumbling, my kids are in." Rod grinned.

"I'd be in, too," Spence joked. "If we get the funds, we'll need all the volunteers we can get."

"Now that's something I can donate. Financially I'm not going to be much help," Kirsten said.

"We're happy to accept any kind of help you want to give." Spence was proving again why he made such a great mayor.

"Great fundraiser, subtle but effective," Lena complimented.

"How are you settling in?" Andy asked her. "Can't be easy coming into a small town like this."

She smiled then flicked her eyes to me before admitting, "I'm still adjusting, but I made the right neighborhood choice." She nodded at Spencer then, with what felt like more meaning, me. The air pressure seemed to drop in the room. She was getting too damn sexy for words.

"Didn't think you'd be here, Gloria," a voice from my past spoke up.

Mine wasn't the only groan issued when we turned to find Rick Orting and his trademark smirk. He'd been my first high school romance and enjoyed bringing that up whenever he came back to town. Calling me by my given name was just one of his ways to establish that he'd known me intimately once. Damn the pressure of prom night. Not that I'd minded getting rid of the annoying virgin thing, but he'd been really juvenile about my surgery scars. It made the experience awkward, but that wasn't the worst thing. He'd gone on to blab about it at school the next week. More specifically that he deserved a medal because of how bad my chest looked. What had been an awkward event became humiliating for me, even if his bragging backfired. I went from being the new girl with the heart thing to the sweet girl with the heart thing wronged by an asshole.

I felt the usual flash of regret and momentary twinge along the scar on my chest at the sight of him. If I were a bigger person, I'd thank him for making me open to the prospect of dating women. My small high school hadn't afforded that option and sexuality was still a taboo topic on television at the time. Without Rick being such an ass, I wasn't sure if I would have agreed when Maggie, my first girlfriend, had asked me out in college. I would have figured it out eventually, but I might have wasted a couple more years dating men had Rick not really turned me off.

"I live here, Rick. What brings you to town?" I was always civil with him so that he wouldn't guess his actions in high school still stung a little.

"Dad's sixtieth. Mom's making a big deal." He glanced up at Spencer as if noticing him standing close to me for the first time. "Damn, Spence, are we dating or something?"

"Go find some other place to play, Dick."

"Rick!" he barked but took a step back when he remembered he'd already received one beat down from Spence after bragging to the wrong person. His motion pushed him into Lena. "Who are you, beautiful lady? New to town?"

"Lena this is Rick. Lena's the new high school principal." I watched her take his hand and regard him. She was trying to place where he belonged in the mix. The forced smile told me she'd guessed it in one.

"That's right, old Willie finally kicked the bucket, huh?" His eyes showed amusement, like the death of our former principal was funny to him. "Remember what a pain in the ass that dude was, Glor? How many times did he catch us trying to sneak away for some alone time?"

"I think it's time for you to find your dad," Andy suggested in his best authoritative voice. He hadn't liked Rick when we were younger, but he'd learned to be diplomatic from a very young age. "Give him my best wishes on his sixtieth." He placed a big palm on Rick's back and pushed to get him moving. Rick had no choice but to take a step or he'd fall.

"We should catch up, Gloria. Go over old times." His smirk was the kind that could make a more violent person stick him with a knife.

I didn't know what he was trying to prove this time. Watching him walk away, I felt glad I wouldn't find out.

"Gloria?" Lena teased while the group was preoccupied with making various comments about Rick. "Not Glorious?"

Her tease untwisted the knot that had formed in my stomach at Rick's presence. She was beginning to like me, and not just because I was her neighbor who gave her coffee or beer every once in a while. She actually liked me. She didn't realize it yet and would more than likely fight against it, but she'd come around.

"Whatever you say, Beatrice," I teased back.

Her scowl made me smile.

Chapter 11

Cassie was the tenth person I'd bumped into while shopping today. It didn't matter what time of day I came into the grocery store, I could expect to spend twenty extra minutes chatting with people. I never minded with Cassie. We'd been friends since high school, and as the large animal vet in town, she had many great patient stories that could double as a comedy routine.

"Two of my favorite people." Rick approached us from the produce aisle.

Cassie grasped my arm. She'd never liked Rick even before he turned out to be a jerk to me. "What are you doing back in town?"

"Dad's birthday. You're coming, right?" As the sheriff, his dad was very popular in town. "You, too, Glory, the party wouldn't be the same without you."

"I'm busy."

"Wait. We should talk." He nodded his head at Cassie like it would get her to leave.

She looked at me, asking if she should. Since this was the second time in three days he'd tried to talk to me, I relented. If he was that determined, he might show up on my doorstep, which would be far worse than dealing with him in a public place. "See you soon, Cass."

"Finally," he said when Cassie pushed her cart around the corner. "I thought I'd never get you alone."

"What do you need, Rick? It's not like we're friends."

"We can be. Just say the word." He smirked and stepped closer to me.

I stepped back to make it clear I wasn't interested.

"Hey, listen, I just realized that, you know, I might have screwed up, you know, hurt you way back. We were good together."

He's just now figuring out he was a hurtful jerk? "We were in high school. Let it go. I have."

He nodded over and over. "That's good to hear. I thought you might be holding my stupidity against me."

"Nope." I knew my unconcerned tone was confusing him. He probably didn't like that I wasn't torn up over him. I did have a bit of a body image issue because of his actions, but I definitely wasn't torn up over him.

"Maybe we could try again? I'm in town for the whole week. We could go out? Have some fun? Just like old times."

I laughed, and it surprised him. Rick was a good looking guy. He'd probably never had anyone turn him down before. He'd certainly never been laughed at when he asked someone out.

"Damn, Glor, take it easy. We could have fun. We always did."

"No, thanks."

"I've changed. We were kids. Give me a chance again."

I stepped past him. I could finish my shopping some other day. "Not interested, Rick. Take care. Say hi to your dad for me."

I didn't bother to look back as I left. He still had a huge ego and rejection always hit those with the biggest egos hardest. The fact that I wasn't emotional about it must only make it smack worse. The spring in my step couldn't feel good either.

* * *

Club Di practically breathed out energy. Music thumped from the live band. Laughter and camaraderie surrounded us. Women danced and drank and had fun everywhere I looked. I made a trip to Denver every two or three months, sometimes just to come this club. I'd made many friends here and found my only dates here. Tonight it felt a little stifling.

I'd planned to crash at my friends' house tonight as I usually did when I visited for the weekend. Now I was thinking of heading home. Having a drink, maybe flirting with a grad student or tourist just didn't appeal. Perhaps it was too soon after my procedure. I was still feeling a little too grateful to be alive for such frivolous activities. Whatever it was, I felt like ordering a coffee so I'd be fine to drive back home.

"What's up with you tonight?" my friend Sheila asked. Her light blue eyes narrowed at me.

"It's loud, hot, and crowded."

"Ahh, our little girl is growing up," Sheila's wife, Christine, crooned. She was in her forties and thought that meant she could meddle in my life.

"Chris has been bitching about the same things since I met her." Sheila leaned in closer. "She hates this place but puts up with it because it's the only place to see our people."

Like we were a different species. That was one sacrifice about small towns, demographics weren't in my favor. Not that I minded. I hadn't given any thought to settling down. Now that my health was no longer a roadblock, I might have to rethink that. Put some more effort into finding someone to date and progressing naturally from there. The friend with benefits situation I'd had for a couple years might not be the answer for me anymore.

"Glory! You didn't say you were coming into town." Speak of the current devil. Miranda, a finance professor at the college, dropped into the chair next to me. She leaned in for a kiss then reached for hugs from my friends. She'd cut her blond hair short, far shorter than

I was used to. The wavy chin length strands looked really cute.

"Just a quick getaway," I said as she turned back to face me.

She wriggled her eyebrows, one of the signs that she'd like to hook up tonight. I could see the anticipation in her hazel eyes. She was always fun, but I didn't feel like it and hadn't for more than six months. Seems like a long time now that I thought about it. If I were smart, I'd take advantage of the opportunity, but something was holding me back.

I shook my head and squeezed her arm. She looked disappointed, but I wasn't her only recreational outlet. She was in an open long distance relationship that satisfied her whenever it was logistically possible.

"At least dance with me." She grabbed my arm and yanked me up. My friends laughed, knowing I had just been complaining about the place and now found myself being dragged farther into it.

Miranda pulled me into her on the dance floor. It didn't matter if the music was upbeat; she liked to dance close, especially for the first dance of the night. Her body felt good against mine. She was about three inches taller and fit nicely. Tonight she was wearing perfume. That was new. New haircut, new perfume, wonder what else was new about her.

"I've missed you," she whispered close to my ear. "You don't come to the city enough."

"It's been a busy year so far."

"Maybe I should come see you?" She leaned back to check my expression. She'd come to Aspen for a few weekends but always ended up leaving early. We both liked to ski, but filling forty-eight hours was a lot of work with a casual friend.

"The slopes open in October." I didn't want to say no. Maybe I'd make a better effort next time we spent the night together. Learn something more about her.

Her thin lips curled, probably glad that I hadn't shut down the idea. No reason to stir things up tonight. "Sure you don't want to come back to my place tonight? It's been a while."

"I'm a little tired. I was just telling Chris and Sheila that I was ready to go home. They were about to razz me when you came up."

"So I saved you? You should reward me." Her eyebrows fluttered again, and I couldn't help but smile.

"You're relentless, Miranda."

"It's charming, right?" She chuckled at her joke, making me laugh with her. She was fun, light and fun.

That had always been enough for me. I was hoping it hadn't lost its appeal permanently. I might be dooming myself to a life of celibacy otherwise.

Chapter 12

Ready to relax for the evening, I stepped out onto my porch. My parents invited me to dinner later, but for now, I planned to breathe in the fresh air and that was all. A scampering of paws on the gravel of my garden path made me look up.

"Kitty!" I exclaimed, waiting for the doggie bullet to hit me.

"He sure likes you," a stranger called out from the street. I tried not to appear disappointed that it wasn't Lena standing there. "Really likes you."

Kitty had taken up his usual spot on the bench that I used as a footrest, leaning part of his body onto my legs. He was such a sweet dog.

"We have a bit of a thing. I'm not ashamed to admit."

"I can tell." The woman smiled brightly when I waved her onto my property. Fender was at her side, like he was usually at Lena's side, but as soon as she started forward, he galloped up to my porch for a rub, too. "Should I be looking for your dognapping van?"

She laughed as she followed Fender onto the porch. "Lena said you were funny."

Really? Lena hadn't ever said that to me. In fact, most of the time it was like prying spikes from a railroad tie to get her to lighten up around me. "Are you visiting?"

"I had to see where my big sis was hiding herself."

Sisters. This would be fun. "I'm Glory. Have a seat, sister of Lena."

"Erika," she supplied, taking Lena's usual seat. She wasn't as tall as her sister, but beauty was a shared trait in that family. "Lena said it was okay to walk the dogs off leash here."

"Sure can. Pet control isn't high on our priority list."

"Small town life, huh?"

Was she curious or taking a jab? "Not for you?"

"I don't think I could live without a mall nearby."

She was serious this time, but it didn't stop me from laughing. "Where do you live?"

"Maryland. This is my first trip to Colorado."

"Are you liking it?"

"So far, so good. It's great to see my sister." The eyes shaped like her sister's flicked over in the direction of Lena's house. "She's settling in. I was secretly hoping that I'd come out here and be asked to help her pack up to move back to Baltimore. I don't see that happening now. Not with two dogs and good friends."

My heart warmed at Erika's words. Lena must have been telling her about our evening porch visits. She tried to be nonchalant about them, showing up sporadically rather than consistently. It didn't fool me. She liked them as much as I did, even on the nights when she left abruptly because I'd irked her in some unknown way. She got irked easily, which should be troubling except that she'd show up sooner or later as if she'd pressed the reset button. It became a little game some nights, wondering if asking a personal question would get my fingers bit off or a vision of her sexy form stalking off my porch.

"There's always room for another Coleridge sister." I tried to tempt Erika.

"Wouldn't that risk your status as a small town?"

"Funny lady." Seems like sarcasm runs in the Coleridge family along with the alluring beauty thing.

She regarded me while accepting the glass of ice tea I poured for her. "I don't have to worry about her, do I?"

I leaned forward, not sure where the concern was coming from. "Why would you?"

She shook her head, a smile playing on her lips. "Is there even a singles' scene here?"

She was worried about her sister's love life? "Are you married?"

"Ten years. Is there?" She was a persistent thing.

"You can find single men here. You might have to find them on the slopes, but they're here."

A laugh burst from her lips. Then she looked guilty for it. "Right."

Right, what? Right, she didn't believe there were single men here? "What's so funny?"

"Why am I not surprised to see my dogs and sister here?" Lena called out from the street. Practiced ease had her slipping the latch on my gate and floating through. "Did they even attempt a real walk before heading straight over here?"

"I opened the door and this one just flat out ran." Erika's finger pointed at what would have been a guilty looking Kitty if dogs could express guilt.

"He does that." Lena stepped onto the porch and set herself into the open spot on the bench next to her dog and my feet. "Hey, Glory. My sister being a pain?"

Erika snorted. "I adore traveling thousands of miles just so you can give me hell."

I chuckled at their sisterly bickering. "She's good."

"See?" Erika jutted her chin at her sister. "Glory was telling me about all the available single men in town."

I coughed, surprised by Erika's taunting tone. "I'm still not sure what she finds so funny about that."

Lena glared at her sister for a moment then looked at me. "She thinks it's funny because she sees more people on her Sunday trips to the mall than she has in this town." She paused seeming to reflect for a moment. "And she knows that men aren't my style."

Men aren't her...Oooh, boy. Either she's a lesbian or celibate. From her sister's earlier laugh, I'd put my money on lesbian. Things just got a little more interesting.

"I thought you guys were friends." Erika shot a confused look at her.

"Doesn't mean we're painting each other's nails and sharing every personal thing, Eri." Lena turned back to me, tentativeness entering her expression. "She has a big mouth. You get used to it after a while."

"Big mouth? I'm not the one who blabbed to Jimmy Lankowitz about my secret crush in high school."

Lena shook her head and sighed. "You were the only one who thought your crush was a secret. Everyone knew, including Jimmy. I just told him to get off his ass if he was going to ask you to prom."

I laughed again. They had the kind of relationship I wished I could have had with a sister or brother. My parents never came through for me, though. As an adult, I could see why they would have been afraid to have another child, but my younger self had been upset at not having siblings.

"Prom," Erika said, shivering at an unshared memory.

"We should go," Lena told her. "I put in a roast when I got home."

"Yum," Erika murmured. "It's so nice not to have to cook for three hungry mouths. I love coming to visit you, sis."

Lena laughed, one single sound. "Lazy bum." She looked at me, all hesitation gone, replaced now by challenge. "Would you like to join us?"

Very much. "Wish I could, but I've got dinner at my parents."

"We're hiking Buckskin Pass on Saturday. You in?" she asked.

"Bleh." I reacted without thinking. Any trail with the word "pass" in it was out for me. That one was about nine miles and didn't even start until about half a mile up. The only trails I could handle were marked short and easy. This one was flat out long and difficult.

The sisters laughed at my reaction, but Lena wasn't about to let me off that easily. "Afraid I'll hike circles around you again?"

"Afraid someone will pilfer all of the baked snacks from my pack when I'm not looking," I teased back. She didn't need to know how accurate her statement was. It was too wonderful having someone think I could do anything everyone else could do.

Erica laughed and pointed an accusing finger at her sister. Lena smiled, tilting her head in appraisal of me. Satisfied, she nodded and stood, grabbing her sister's arm to get her moving.

"Have fun at your padres tonight."

"Nice meeting you, Glory."

"You, too, Erika. Stop by before you leave us."

"Will do." She waved and followed after her sister and the dogs.

I watched the sway of Lena's hips as they retreated up the garden path. Would her being gay make the attraction worse or better? Worse, definitely. She was still my neighbor and my friend, somewhat reluctantly at times, but a friend, nonetheless.

My hot, gay, neighbor, friend.

Chapter 13

The beer sat on the table unopened. I stared longingly at it. Perhaps Lena wasn't coming by tonight. It was getting a little ridiculous how much I enjoyed these evening visits. Especially since we didn't always agree on everything and she wasn't exactly easy to get to know. But I liked seeing her almost every day. Liked the comfort I felt at having her on the porch with me.

I looked over at her house. Not much was visible now that all the leaves had come in. I couldn't spot her car, but she might have pulled it into the garage. Mei's car was in my driveway, which could be the reason Lena hadn't come over. I was wondering what I'd say if she ever guessed why Mei's car was in my driveway some nights. I didn't feel right about lying to her, but it wasn't my right to tell her about Mei and Spencer.

Grabbing the full bottle, I rose from my seat, ready to head inside. Surely I could find something on television to fight the disappointment.

"I found out something today."

My heart actually leapt at the sound of the voice I'd been waiting for. She'd made it just in time. I watched her walk toward me. She seemed a little off, her gait hesitant, her expression a mixture of annoyance and guilt. When she reached the porch, I retook my seat, placing her beer back on the side table. She glanced at it then back at me before sighing and dropping into the chair next to me.

"What were you saying?"

She sighed again. "I found out that I'm an asshole today."

Frowning then smiling, I asked, "You found out that someone thinks you're an asshole, or you found out you're actually an asshole?"

She smacked my arm lightly. "You're a riot."

"You can't give me an opening like that." I spread my hands out. "How did the asshole discussion come about?"

She turned to face me. "I was having lunch with Jennifer today."

This should be interesting. Jennifer was second only to Terry on the school board for gossip. Some meetings we barely started on time because it was impossible to shut those two up.

"She told me about your heart condition."

My head snapped away, staring out at the street. I let a breathy huff escape. "Oh."

"If I'd known I wouldn't have given you a hard time about not being in shape. You should have said something, told me to shut up or something." She let out a frustrated growl when I didn't respond. "Listen, I'm trying to apologize to you."

I couldn't explain why anger took hold of me. I wasn't angry that Jennifer told her. I wasn't angry that anyone else in town knew. I just liked so much that Lena didn't. "No, you're not."

Her shoulders shot off the chair. "Yes, I am."

I took a deep breath and released it. My anger dissipated into frustration, two emotions I rarely felt. "No, you're trying to get me to give you a break because you didn't realize I was defective and needed to pity me instead of being an asshole. Well, too bad, you are an asshole. Telling someone she isn't in shape isn't kind. It doesn't matter if she's a defect or not." I paused, letting that sink in. "Lucky for you, I like assholes."

Silence stretched between us. I tried to deal with these foreign emotions while she was trying to reconcile the laid-back Glory she'd been getting to know with the raging bitch I appeared to be now.

"Damn, you're tough."

"But in a defective way, right?"

She squinted, pulling back as if the notion offended her. I should let her off the hook, but it bugged me that she felt she had to apologize for teasing me because she found out I had a legitimate reason for the thing she'd been teasing me about. I should have known this day would come. Too many people knew that I had a heart condition. Very few actually knew the extent, but some knew it was life threatening. It was just a matter of time before someone blabbed to Lena. Didn't mean I wanted to deal with it, though.

"I don't need your sympathy. In fact, I find it refreshing that you don't treat me with kid gloves like everyone else because they're afraid I'm going to have a heart attack if they say something that upsets me."

Concern fluttered across her expression. "But I seriously thought you had a conditioning problem."

"I do." It was doctor allowed, but I did.

"One that you should do something about, I mean."

"And now you know I can't. So, what? You're going to stop teasing me about things?"

"No." She huffed, tightening her lips. She was used to me being even-tempered, had probably expected me to tell her that everything was fine and not to worry about it. My reaction must be twisting her around.

"Sure." I focused on the forest, listening for the sounds of animal life and the breeze fluttering through the leaves. I wished I'd gone inside before she came over. We could use her reset button for tomorrow night. Maybe then I'd be in a better mood for her pity.

"I'm sorry," she tried. "I just wanted to let you know that I realized I was being a jerk to you about being out of shape, and I had no right to be. I wanted to tell you, that's all."

"So you told me." I picked up my empty bottle and stood from the chair.

"Where are you going?"

"I'm tired."

"You're mad." She grabbed my arm to keep me from leaving. "I didn't mean to upset you, but I felt like such a jerk today at lunch. I couldn't believe I'd been so cruel to you."

"You haven't been. Don't you get it? Why do you think I keep letting you come over here every night when you're not exactly the warmest person I've ever met? Do you think I have such bad self-esteem that I'd allow someone to dig at me on a regular basis while I continued to try to make her like me?" I started laughing. I knew that would throw her off, probably tick her off, but I couldn't help it. "I actually like the way your mind works. You like trying to figure people out, but you can't stand it when someone does the same to you. Well, dear, you've met your match."

Her eyes glowered. If it were anatomically possible, steam would be coming out of her ears. She probably didn't realize that she was still holding onto my arm. The warm fingers contracted but didn't let go.

"You come over here almost every night, mostly we do well, but sometimes you leave after I've said something to tick you off. I don't take it to heart, and neither do you, because here you come again on the next night. I get you, and that bugs the hell out of you, doesn't it?"

"You don't know what you're talking about."

"Believe that all you like."

She released my arm and pushed up from the chair. Her menacing glare expressed more than her silent mouth. She started to say something then stormed off the porch.

"At least tonight you're not the only one ticked off," I said as she hit the gravel pathway. "And I know you well enough to know that if I say, 'you'll be back tomorrow,' you won't no matter how much you want to head over here because you're that stubborn. So, I'll just tell you that I'll be here tomorrow if you feel like stopping by." I watched her back turn the corner and disappear behind the trees. "Bye, Lena!"

As annoyed as I was, I entered my house with a wide smile.

From the Journal of Lena Coleridge:

Smug little attitude. Damn her. I wanted to wipe that all-knowing grin right off her face. Telling me I'm an asshole when all I wanted to do was apologize for being so insensitive to her condition. Not that it's a condition. Just that, hell, I don't know. I just felt bad for being an ass, and she sure as hell didn't make it easy for me to apologize. Had my number right from the get go and hid it all this time. I wonder what else she's hiding.

Calling herself a defect. I felt like shaking her until she stopped thinking that way. Clearly that's a sore subject for her, but dammit, all I wanted to do was let her know I wasn't a heartless bitch.

When she told me I'd be back tomorrow then somehow knew that by telling me what to do I wouldn't do it, I wanted to smack her. Then kiss her. No! Not kiss her. What am I thinking? Why would I want to kiss such a know-it-all pain in the ass neighbor that I see every day with her tight ass and young, firm body—oh, hell! Rip out this page. If that woman ever figured out I'd even thought those things, much less written them down, she'd hang that over my head for all eternity.

Note to self: check real estate and job listings for some other beautiful ski town, maybe in another state.

Chapter 14

When Superintendent Terry called another special session of the school board a week before summer break, I was surprised. The last time he did this, he'd told us about William's stroke. I hoped it wasn't the same kind of bad news.

Terry looked grim but not pale like he had the last time. We took our seats, nodding to each other. This wasn't an open session, so it was just the five of us. Everyone else looked as confused as I did.

"Thank you for making it to this special session," Terry began, speaking into a microphone out of habit. When we all grinned, he leaned back and addressed us again. "My office has taken several complaints over the past month, and it's time that we address them."

"Complaints about what?" Joel asked.

"Our newest principal."

"What's she doing now? Making the kids who misbehave peel potatoes?" Mitch joked.

"She is still continuing with her harsh punishments, but these complaints are far more serious." Terry cleared his throat and looked nervous for a moment. He seemed to make up his mind. "Some parents have complained that Ms. Coleridge has pushed a homosexual agenda on their children."

"What?" Jennifer spoke up first as every one of us popped off the backs of our chairs and leaned forward.

"I've had more than twenty phone calls with parents over the past two weeks, and I found them very disturbing."

"What are they saying she did?" Joel asked.

"She called an assembly to talk about sexual orientation. The parents are extremely upset as you can imagine. We've made a decision on this board to have parents sign off on sex ed courses prior to students taking them. None of these parents signed off on this and they're livid."

"Wait a minute," I started but was cut off by Jennifer.

"She what? And she's taking that opportunity to teach kids about homosexuality? Is she, you know? I mean, that seems highly inappropriate."

"Hold on," I tried again but was no more successful.

"She is. I brought her into my office today and asked her." Terry looked proud of his investigative skills.

"You did what?" I slammed my hands down on the desk, getting everyone's attention. "What made you think you could ask an employee a personal question like that, Terry?"

"I had to find out if these rumors were true."

"What rumors? Parents getting bits of information from kids who have the attention span of patio furniture?" I glared at each of them, my stare down finishing with Terry. "Did you know that asking a question like that could bring a sexual harassment suit against you?"

"Don't be absurd. I didn't come onto her."

"Having your boss corner you about your sexual orientation and feeling like you have no choice but to answer could be construed as making her work environment hostile." It pays to have a best friend who's an attorney.

He waved his hands. "You weren't there, Glory. She didn't seem upset by my question. She was fine telling me she was gay. I didn't go into details with her until we figured out what to do, but we may have to consider starting another candidate search over the summer."

I was so shocked that I could barely form a thought. Terry had just called for a vote to terminate Lena based on rumors. "Stop it," my mouth said for my brain. "Did you ask Lena what the assembly was about, or did you just take the parents' word for it?"

Terry lowered his eyes. Just as I suspected. He didn't once think the parents might be lying or at the very least exaggerating. Mitch blinked several times, the thought just occurring to him as well. The glassy stare Jennifer was showing indicated that she wasn't even tuned in anymore. Joel's brow pinched, his eyes solemn as he waited everyone out.

"You all know that Lena is my neighbor and she's become my friend. She's become yours as well, hasn't she, Jen?"

"Well, yes," she agreed after a long hesitation.

"Last week, Lena mentioned an assembly she held on tolerance and what it means to be open minded. She told me that she went through issues that involve racial, gender, body type, sexual orientation, and religious differences. Her goal was to make it clear that intolerance and bullying would not be allowed."

Their reactions all differed. Terry's eyes popped open. Mitch began nodding, his hands lifting off the desk. Jennifer's glassy stare didn't alter. If she was evening listening, she wasn't registering it. Joel, the quiet one, the one who usually held to traditions, gave a minute smile, his eyes glittering with interest.

"Did those parents mention anything about these other topics, Terry? Did they tell you that she was teaching sex ed, or that she was teaching what it means to be intolerant toward homosexuality?"

He squinted, looking like he was experiencing constipation. "They seemed concerned that she was teaching them about being homosexual."

I shook my head, ashamed that he'd take the word of emotional parents over his own employee. "She wasn't, but she would tell kids that it's not right to treat homosexuals any differently."

The end of year assembly had been a safe topic that Lena and I could discuss last week in the wake of me biting her head off. I still felt bad about it and had apologized for lashing out at her. She didn't seem to be treating me differently. She'd been annoyed with me in the past and I never held it against her, but this had been an irrational reaction on my part. Having the assembly subject matter to mull over had helped get us past the initial awkwardness and back on the friendship track.

Terry glanced down at his notepad. "That's not what these parents said."

"Is Rebecca, the mother of the boy who tormented the other boy because he thinks he's gay, one of those parents?" At Terry's guilty look, I continued, "We know she has motivation to have Lena removed since her son is the only senior who is waitlisted for college. Her son is a homophobe and if she's defending his behavior, she is as well. I doubt that Lena has made her sexual identity known to her students, but if Rebecca knows, she'd be very motivated to get rid of her."

"Did you know?" Terry asked me in an accusatory manner.

"That's not really your business, Terry."

"It would have been nice to have a heads up is all. This isn't a big city, Glory. Some of these people haven't had much exposure to a controversial subject like this. Parents are obviously concerned."

"So we educate them," I said. "I can't believe you're actually considering firing a woman who has brought in the best test results this school has ever seen, gotten every senior who wanted to go to college into college, cut down on truancies, eliminated vandalism, and gotten her kids involved in community outreach programs. You're proposing we fire her because her sexuality makes some parents uneasy? Don't you understand how wrong that is?"

"Glory, come on, I was responding to parent complaints. You know we have to take those seriously."

"Terry, you come on. You know parents are lions when it comes to their kids and have no backbone for discipline anymore. If their kids whine, they turn on the educators because they don't want to take responsibility. I'm betting that more than half of those complaints came from parents who didn't even know what the assembly was about. They heard it through the town grapevine and got all riled up for nothing."

Mitch shrugged. "That does happen, Ter."

"Why didn't you just ask Lena about the assembly? You could have stopped this before any other complaints came in."

Terry's shoulders fell. "I should have spoken to her about it, but I was shocked to learn that she'd been teaching sex education, specifically homosexual education, to a bunch of teenagers."

I shook my head and sighed. "Sex education should include everything involving sex, sexually transmitted diseases, and pregnancy no matter the sexual orientation of the students. We might be opening ourselves up to lawsuits if it isn't comprehensive." Knowing we wouldn't resolve this topic tonight, I shifted back to the original reason we were here. "Putting that aside, we have the best damn principal this district has ever seen under contract and we're not letting her go because some people might have a problem with her sexual orientation."

"I agree with Glory," Joel said. "Lena has performed beautifully. My kids have never been more excited about school. She also seems like a wonderful gal, so I don't see what all this fuss is about."

My eyes widened. Joel had originally voted against her. He was also the oldest person on the board, so it was a little shocking to see him so open to her sexuality. Of course that was prejudiced of me to say.

"She does bring in results," Jennifer said, but she didn't seem as convinced as I was.

"Fine, we'll table this, but I will be asking for an outline of all assembly topics in the future."

I nodded, conceding that it would be a good idea for the board to know what was being taught outside the standard course curriculum. It also helped that Lena always made extensive outlines for her assemblies, so it wouldn't be any more work for her.

When I left the room, I felt my heart rate slow. I hadn't realized that I'd gotten so worked up, but I was definitely put off by their complete disregard for her privacy and ability to do her job. They'd never suggested that we fire the two teachers on staff who were gay, but they were both locals. Perhaps that was what this was all about. Lena was still considered an outsider. The board might be experiencing buyers' remorse with the decision to hire her. Maybe once the summer passed and the new school year began, they'd start thinking of her as a local and start extending more support.

Chapter 15

Christine and Sheila pulled me through the doors of Club Di. I was supposed to be spending the weekend helping Christine paint their nursery. I hadn't counted on an outing to the club when they'd called with the pregnancy news and request for help, but I should have known they'd want a break after working all day.

Christine went up to the bar to grab some drinks as Sheila and I found a table. Taking a seat, I couldn't stop the déjà vu feeling. I'd thought a change of scenery from my place would be good, but seeing my friends, coming to this club, hearing the same music, seeing the same wait staff and most of the same people, it wasn't the change I'd been looking for. I hadn't really noticed that I'd needed a change, just craved a little something different for the weekend. Now that I had it, I realized it wasn't the kind of difference I was looking for. The last time this happened to me, I'd left Philly and moved back to Aspen. I hoped this mood of mine wasn't looking for that kind of change again.

"Thanks again for helping out," Sheila said as we settled in for what would probably be a three hour stint here.

"I'm happy to. The room's looking great. Maybe before I leave, Chris and I can put together the crib and changing table."

"That would be so great. She's been worried that we wouldn't have everything done by the time the critter gets here." She rubbed her now prominent belly without really noticing it.

"Shouldn't you stop calling it a critter soon?"

"If you saw the last sonogram, you'd call it a critter, too." She smiled with a wistfulness that all new parents have.

Christine joined us, setting our drinks on the table. "Did you call Miranda?"

"I forgot," I said, not terribly broken up about it. I hadn't even thought of it to be honest. Nothing about my current dry spell bothered me.

"Call her now," Sheila prompted.

"That's okay. Not really into it."

They exchanged an amused look. "You're ready to fall in love, aren't you?"

My eyes popped wide, head pushing back to look at her. "What are you talking about?"

"Maybe she already has," Christine told her wife.

"Maybe," she agreed.

"Are you talking about me?" I asked, confused.

"Do you realize that this is the third time you've been in here and not hooked up with Miranda? Are you getting some back home?" Christine asked.

"Some little ski bunny come into town for a few weeks and you grabbed her while you could?" Sheila guessed.

My head shook at their warped view of my life. They'd visited me in Aspen for ski weekends many times and never once did I bring home a ski bunny. They liked to think I was getting more than my once every three month sessions with Miranda. They were firm believers that sex was good for every part of a woman. Apparently, they didn't care where I got it just so long as I did.

"Nothing so Lifetime Movie Channel, I assure you."

"You don't miss sex?"

I started to deflect the question, but I must have run out of energy painting the room. "Not really."

"Miranda isn't the one, then?" Sheila deflated before my eyes. "We'd been hoping that after a couple years of this 'no-strings' arrangement, you'd realize how good you both were together. Guess that's not happening."

"She's lovely," I said. She was, just not for me. "I like her a lot, but I haven't given a lot of thought to the rest of my life."

I didn't tell them why. They might think it weird that I'd never thought of a future with marriage and children. Until my junior year, my future always had an expiration date. I never focused on it, was always hopeful that yet another medical advancement would intervene, but I had to believe it was why I'd never envisioned life past college. The valve replacement in high school allowed me to think of an adult future, but I'd concentrated on my career. With that now in hand, it might be time to start considering whether or not I'd be growing old alone rather than wondering if I'd grow old at all. Or I could just start my cat collection sooner rather than later.

"Does she know?" Sheila asked.

"I'm the diversion in our relationship. She definitely knows."

They turned to look at each other with raised eyebrows. I thought I'd mentioned that Miranda had a long-term relationship that she'd turn permanent as soon as her girlfriend got tenure somewhere. Why she hadn't already moved out to Florida to be with her girlfriend, I wasn't sure. I do know she loved the mountains, so maybe that was it. Either way, I never had a chance at a future with her, which was probably why I'd picked her.

"That's not upsetting to you?" Chris asked.

"Not even a little. I told you it was a casual thing. I'm happy with that." I was and always had been. After being disappointed by the lack of involvement with my first two girlfriends, I began to seek out casual. It worked best for my lifestyle and fit well with my attitude. I hadn't been disappointed in ten years.

"But not anymore, otherwise you'd be visiting more than once every three months, right?"

"I hadn't realized it was that little, honestly."

"If you say so. We obviously want you to be happy. With the baby on the way, we've been thinking about the future a lot more." Chris said, reaching over to rub her wife's belly.

"I'm happy, and happy that you're happy."

They nodded, seeming to take that in stride. They were good friends, comfortable friends. I liked having them in my life, but I knew things would change when the baby arrived. I doubt I'd use them as my crash pad once the critter came. At least not until the baby slept through the night.

"How come every time we mention her, she shows up?" Sheila said then nodded at something over my shoulder.

I turned to see Miranda walking into the bar. She went to place an order, saying hello to several regulars on her way. Her eyes met mine and a big smile creased her face. She waved then pointed at the bar, raising a finger. When she grabbed a beer, she came straight for us. She was beautiful, that was certain, but she never made my heart pound.

"Hey, Glor, hi, guys, what a wonderful surprise." She leaned down to kiss me hello and hugged my friends. "Mind if I join you? I came in for a beer, but I'd love to hang out with friends."

"Sure." I pushed the chair next to me away from the table for her. "We just ordered. Want something to eat?"

"Not tonight, thanks. It's getting so hot these days. I never feel like eating at night."

"Try being pregnant in this weather," Sheila groaned, which set off a long discussion about how the preparations were coming for the baby.

By the time Sheila stopped with the baby news, we'd finished dinner. I'd heard it all when they called to tell me, so I barely paid attention. I was enjoying the atmosphere and the light touches from Miranda. She really had been good for me. A lot healthier than my first girlfriend in college, and a lot nicer than the three since. It was almost too bad we couldn't be a couple. Not that we'd be right for each other even if she were available, but she was easy to be with.

"Let's dance." Her breath was hot on my ear.

I recognized the look in her eyes. She wanted to hook up tonight. I wasn't sure that was such a good idea. I'd often come in here with Sheila and Christine only to have them shove me at Miranda for the night. Seeing as the nursery was my former guest room, maybe it wouldn't be a bad idea to head to Miranda's tonight.

I let her lead me to the dance floor. After using my arm all day, it was nice to work out other muscles. We danced well together, always had. She was really fun to be with, and the sex was pretty good, too. Had my cavalier attitude about visiting to hook up with her been my subconscious telling me that we'd never work out? More likely it was that my energy level had been so low prior to my stent procedure that sex was the last thing on my mind.

The way she looked and moved now, I had to think that was the reason. I could definitely see getting together with her tonight. I envisioned the look on her face when she came. The memory had me pressing closer.

Her eyes widened, a sneaky grin creeping across her face. "Missed you," she whispered right before she leaned down and kissed me.

I returned the kiss without a lot of enthusiasm. If I had one complaint, it would be our kisses. They never curled my toes. To be honest, they weren't that great. She wasn't entirely to blame. It takes two to make a great kiss, but we hadn't had one yet. I never knew what her tongue was trying to do with my mouth. It wasn't awful, but I'd definitely had better.

"Wanna play tonight?" she asked when she broke the kiss, grasping my hips and gyrating against me. The contact pushed a surge of warmth through me. "Come on, Glor, it's been forever."

It had been forever. I leaned in to kiss her again, hoping like I always did that it would be different this time. It wasn't, but my friends' words rang in my head. It had been a long time, and I had a wonderful woman who wanted to have sex with me. I should take advantage of the opportunity.

She smiled widely when I tilted back, knowing she'd convinced me. She tugged on my hand. As I turned to go with her, I caught sight of a familiar face. I stopped, the familiarity paralyzing me for a moment.

Miranda pulled again, taking me out of view. Moments later we were standing in front of my friends' table. They smiled and winked at me as she explained that she'd be taking me home, but they could have me back tomorrow. Before I had a chance to say anything, I was being dragged out the door.

My last view before the door closed was of Lena's wide eyes and open mouth.

Chapter 16

When I turned into my driveway after work, Lena was already sitting on my front porch. Normally she wouldn't be walking by for another hour, but I could tell she wanted to talk. I'd seen it in her eyes on Saturday night before I left the club.

I tried to put her shocked reaction out of my head as soon as I cleared the doors. It worked until we'd gotten to Miranda's place. She'd pulled me toward her bedroom, but instead of getting wrapped up in her eagerness, all I could see was Lena's face. Pushing it aside proved impossible. I had to call an end to the evening before Miranda had a chance to undress. She'd been really upset, and I couldn't blame her. I also couldn't go through with our plans when I kept thinking of someone else.

That someone shot out of her chair as soon as I got out of my car. Something just shy of fury propelled her to the edge of the porch while I grabbed my briefcase from the back seat. She barely waited until I had closed the door and started toward the house.

"Why didn't you tell me?"

"Tell you what? And hello, by the way."

Her hands propped on her hips, shaking her head at me. "You know damn well what I'm talking about. I've been pouring out my life story to you over the past couple of months, and you sit there saying nothing. Imagine my surprise when I find out we're the same?"

"We are?" I asked, confused. I wasn't as hotheaded as she was. I didn't have the patience for kids that she did. I wasn't reluctant about living in a small town like she was. I could probably name ten more significant differences, but she had a point to make.

"Yes! When I saw you on Saturday night I nearly choked. How could you not tell me you're a lesbian?"

I made it to my front door and tossed my briefcase inside. In the front closet, I found the cooler and checked to see if it was stocked. Pulling it outside, I opened it and offered her a beer. She glared at me then at the beer before relenting and ripping it out of my hands. I tried not to smile at her ire, but it was pretty cute how worked up she could get about things.

I took a seat and thought about my response. "Have I told you that artichokes are my favorite vegetable? Or how I wish they'd ban snowboarding from half the runs on Ajax and Snowmass? Or that I'm an only child who wished every day of her life that she had a sister or brother?"

"What are you talking about? I'm pissed at you here." She had yet to take a seat, but she had opened the beer. Baby steps.

I waited for her to stop pacing and return her attention to me. "I'm trying to prove that being a lesbian is only one facet of me. Since I'm not in a relationship, it doesn't even register on the scale of things that define me. It has nothing to do with our friendship, nor does it have to do with the fact that we can enjoy an evening together without talking about sexual preferences. We don't know a lot about each other, Lena. Why should that be one of the first things I tell you about myself?"

"Because you were lying to me this whole time."

I mentally rolled my eyes. If I thought actually rolling my eyes wouldn't get me punched, I'd probably do that. "Omitting something isn't a lie. I didn't deceive you or misrepresent myself. Everyone has a right to privacy. You choose to tell most people you're gay. I choose not to. I don't think poorly of your decision. You have no right to think poorly of mine."

She blew out a long breath, the stiffness in her shoulders easing. "But you knew I was having a hard time in this small town. I told you that. You knew I'd find comfort in knowing that there was at least one lesbian that I knew."

"No, I didn't. Why would knowing I'm a lesbian make you feel more comfortable with me as your friend? Are you saying that lesbians make better friends? That's prejudiced. I take offense to that. Some of my best friends aren't lesbians." I tried to inject a little levity into the discussion but could see that she wasn't ready to let it go. "You're just ticked that I didn't tell you."

"I'm ticked that you hide it from the whole town, using Spence as your beard."

I laughed. If only she knew. "I don't use him at all. We're friends. We tell anyone who wants to listen that we're friends. You and I hang out as much as Spence and I hang out. I'm not using you, and I don't give a damn if the town decides that I'm dating you like some have decided I date Spence."

"You're telling me that when I see you at Spencer's side at some functions you're not hoping that everyone in town thinks you two are dating?"

"I'm telling you I don't give a damn what they think. I like Spence. He's a guy who has a lot of work functions to attend. He takes his mom or his buddy James as often as we attend together. He knows I'm gay. I'm not using him."

Lena dropped onto the bench in front of me. "I just wish you'd told me."

"How did my not telling you affect you at all? Did it hurt you? Did it upset you? Or was it that you thought you had a right to my privacy so that you wouldn't feel so vulnerable?"

She glared at me. Guessed right. Or at least partially right. "How do you always manage to tick me off like no one else before?"

"I'm special."

She laughed then went back to looking mad. "You should have told me. We didn't have to analyze it, but saying 'oh, you're gay? So am I' would have been nice to hear."

"See a time machine around here?"

She made a loud frustrated sound then stood. "There's no winning with you."

"Especially since I didn't know we were competing."

One last sigh pushed from her lips. "Next time I tell you something I like, you better tell me if you like it, too."

She was relenting. A new action for her, at least as far as I was concerned. I'd get her to unwind at some point. Years from now probably, but I'd do it.

From the Journal of Lena Coleridge:

How did I not see it? A real lesbian—practically an endangered species around these parts—living next door, and I had no clue. How stupid am I? Not that she gives any hints. She doesn't look at women as far as I've seen, not even a discreet check. I was guilty of that just last week. Didn't matter that they were gorgeous celebrities, I checked them out when they took that table next to us. But Glory? Nope, not even a fleeting glance. Maybe she's really into that woman from the bar. God, how rare would that be? A partner that's so into you she doesn't notice there are other women around. Wouldn't that be something?

Still, I should have picked up something from her. Usually that isn't a problem for me. Spotted the two I met last week from a mile away. Joanna and Brandy, too bad they're too juvenile to be real friends, but it's good to know others exist in this town. I thought I might be the only single one here. Crazy thing is, they let loose with the goods on a few others but not one mention of Glory. Could be they don't know her. As small as this place is, I am finding out it is actually possible not to know everyone.

All that makes it worse that Erika tells her about me and my frickin' lesbian neighbor doesn't offer, "Yeah? So am I." Who wouldn't do that? We live next door to each other. We spend many nights having a drink together or walking my dogs. She knew she had a lesbian—one of very few in town—living next door to her, and she didn't think I'd want to know about her? What is wrong with that woman? It's like she lives to irritate me.

And now, the smart, beautiful, easy going, funny, put together, so damn sexy woman next door is—crap on crackers—no longer a safe, impossible, out of bounds fantasy.

Chapter 17

My front door opened just as I was pulling dinner out of the oven. I set it down on a trivet and leaned back to get a glimpse of my visitor. It was probably my mom. She telecommuted from home and liked any excuse to get out of the house for an hour.

"I made tamale casserole," I announced.

"Yum," Mei responded unenthusiastically. She stood just inside my front door, suitcase in hand, despondent look on her face.

"Hey," I greeted, eyeing the suitcase. "What's going on?"

"I told him," she whispered, her brown eyes filling with tears.

I waited for her to continue, not wanting to guess. Taking her suitcase, I freed up her arms for a much needed hug. She clung to me for a long while before stepping back and letting out a shuddering breath. She looked around my house, a place she knew as well as her own, but today she looked as if it was all new to her. With a huge sigh, she dropped onto the couch.

"I asked Andy for a divorce."

I nodded, sitting next to her and offering her my arms again. She came to me, huddled close and cried for a good long while. As unattached as she was to Andy and had been for three years, I knew she'd be heartbroken when she finally called it off. I could tell it surprised her how much it hurt.

"He was," she started then let out another big sob, "he didn't seem to care."

"Of course he did, Mei," I assured her. "You know how Andy reacts to things. It may take a while before it sinks in."

"He almost seemed relieved, Glor, really."

I didn't want to comment on that. Andy wasn't entirely clueless. He'd probably felt his wife pulling away from him this past year, even if he wasn't home much and paid more attention to work than he did to his wife.

"I came home to an empty house like always." Mei rubbed her eyes and pressed back against the couch. "I was making dinner when he got there. He dropped his briefcase, grunted hello, and dashed into the bathroom for a shower. By the time he came back into the kitchen, dinner had been sitting there for thirty minutes. He grabbed his keys and was saying goodbye before I even knew what was going on."

I could picture the whole thing. I'd witnessed him do the same thing in the past when I'd been over for dinner. He always claimed that he forgot Mei had invited me over. He'd have a tennis court reserved or a tee time to get to or cases to review on his docket. By the time he got home it was usually midnight, and he'd go straight to bed. That had been their home life for many years. Even before Spencer came into the picture, I'd made subtle hints that perhaps she should examine what made her most happy. I never believed that an empty home life did.

"I grabbed his arm to keep him there." She blew her nose on an offered tissue. "He looked so surprised that I wouldn't let him leave. I tried to break it to him easily. Tried to say that we'd been growing apart for years, but I couldn't do it. I just told him that I wanted a divorce. He looked at me for a long time. Then he nodded his head. That's it. No argument, no asking me why."

"Oh, Mei. I'm sorry. I know this hurts."

"It sucks."

"Big time," I agreed.

"I guess I should be happy he didn't yell and get upset and demand to know why. I'm not sure I could have stopped myself from telling him about Spence."

We'd talked about this a few times. We thought it would be best for her not to tell him about Spencer. It seemed like she'd be kicking him when he was down. Andy didn't need to know that she'd fallen in love with someone else.

"You aren't leaving him because of Spence."

She glanced away before fixing her stare back on me. "You're right. I should have done this years ago."

I didn't comment or nod. She didn't need me telling her that.

"I've wasted so much of my life in a nowhere marriage."

"You don't know that. You weren't held back. Andy is a good man. Not the right man for you, but a good man."

She took in a deep shuddering breath and let it go. "Can I stay with you for a while? I could stay at the office, but I don't feel like being alone yet. I definitely don't want to stay with my parents. I can't tell them yet. They're going to be so disappointed."

"Stay as long as you like."

"You sure? I won't be crowding you? No visits from Miranda this week?"

No more visits from her ever. She still hadn't forgiven me for leaving her place a couple weeks ago. It wasn't like we'd gotten past kissing that night. I shut it down before she could get all hot and bothered. I'd tried texting her a couple times, hoping we could stay friends, but I guess friends with no benefits wasn't the type of friendship she was looking for.

"I think we're done."

"Really?" Mei leaned toward me, happy to concentrate on something other than her own failed marriage. "Did she finally decide to move to Florida and be with the woman she claims to love?"

I couldn't hold in my laughter. Separation seems to have made my sweet best friend snippy. "I don't know what she plans to do, but it wasn't right for me anymore."

"No more Denver sex weekends?"

We both laughed at that one. "I'll eventually have to go back if I ever want sex again, but not any time soon, no."

"You could always start pursuing Molly. You know she's had a thing for you for years."

"Oh, stop it," I chided, thinking of the extremely butch backpacking guide employed by one of the outdoor gear shops in town. She was nice enough, but definitely not my type. I wasn't hers either, but in a small town with limited single lesbians, choosey isn't an option. She asked me out occasionally, testing to see if I would change my mind. I always encouraged her toward the three single women I knew. Joanna and Brandy, the attractive ski instructors, or Vivian, the gorgeous interior designer, probably wouldn't agree to a date any more than I would, but only because they tended to get involved with tourists or head to Denver for their liaisons. Molly wasn't into tourists anymore. She was looking for permanence. Even if her look wasn't my thing, her intensity would never have meshed with me.

"Are you upset about this? You and Miranda have been together for a couple years."

"Not really. I never really considered us together. I always assumed I'd get a text telling me we couldn't get together anymore because she'd finally gotten a full commitment from her girlfriend."

"I'm sorry it's over, even if you never considered it on."

I squeezed her arm. "Thanks. You hungry? Tamale casserole."

She grinned for the first time. "That does sound good. I'll cook tomorrow night."

I shrugged, letting her know we'd do whatever she needed to do to get her through this time. The fact that she hadn't called Spence yet told me that she was going to play this separation period the best way she could. Running straight to Spence's arms might not be the best decision she could make in a small town. I was glad to see that she hadn't lost her common sense.

Chapter 18

A week passed before I could enjoy an evening on my porch. Mei was now set up in a house sitting situation. We had a lot of out of town clients who were happy to have a trustworthy guest in their winter homes. She was doing a lot better, admitting that the marriage had been over for years, ready to move on with her life. I was very proud of her for making that decision and equally proud of her that she hadn't moved into Spencer's. They probably both wanted to do that, but they were being respectful. This separation was a good time to let Mei finalize things before she jumped head first into the relationship she really wanted.

"Hey, stranger," Lena called out as she approached my driveway.

My heart thumped and my stomach fluttered at the sight of her. I hadn't realized that I'd missed seeing her over the past week. We'd gone days without seeing each other before, but this time, it felt different.

"Hi."

The dogs reached me first. I patted each one before they took their spots on the porch. They made me grin. Whether Lena planned to stay or not, the dogs were. She looked at them and shook her head before taking her usual seat. I offered her some lemonade and we sat quietly for a while.

"Is Mei okay?"

I looked over at her, studying her expression. "You heard?"

"I didn't realize how small this town was."

Yes, it was, especially when one resident had a big mouth. Andy hadn't even waited a day to tell his buddies. He also hadn't stayed home the night Mei had asked for a divorce. He'd gone off to his poker night and apparently suffered diarrhea of the mouth. Mei started getting calls at the office the next day. We'd left early so that Mei could take out her anger at Andy's insensitivity on the weeds in my yard. Afterwards, we'd gone to her house and packed her up. She made a clean break, and soon, I'd encourage her to file the papers.

"She's getting through it."

"Give her my best, will you?" She took a sip of lemonade and glanced back out at the trees. "Divorce is no fun."

I turned, interested. She sounded like she was speaking from experience. "Were you married?"

"Once." At my raised eyebrows, she added, "Not to a man."

Her standoffishness started to make sense. It didn't sound like her marriage was all hearts and fairy tale endings.

"I'm sorry it didn't work out."

"I'm not anymore. I hope Mei can get to that realization, too."

"I think she will." I didn't mention that it was Mei who'd wanted and needed the divorce.

"You've never been married?"

I grinned at her. I wondered if she realized this was the first really personal question she'd asked me. I had just asked her the same thing, but she almost never brought up topics from our pasts. "Nope."

"Not the marrying kind?" she teased.

"Never really thought about it."

"The woman from the bar? She's not your Ms. Right?"

I laughed, but her confused expression made me stop. "No. We were friends. I was her diversion."

"You're not anymore?"

"No. I hope to be her friend again, but the diversion is done."

"Didn't bring her enough baked goods?"

I shot a sly look at her. "I've never baked anything for her."

"Save those for special people only?"

She thought she was teasing, but I answered honestly. "You can tell a lot about a person from her baked goods. She and I were never that close."

An involuntary sound left her mouth. She was surprised by it and chose to lean down and pet Fender for the distraction. I smiled, knowing I'd just tossed a flirting lob her way. It was dangerous territory, I knew, but sometimes I liked testing boundaries.

"Did you find anyone special at Club Di?"

She snickered softly. "About twenty fourteen-year-olds. God, were we really that young in college?" She glanced at me. "What am I saying? You still are."

"Hey, I'm way past my teen drama years, thank you very much."

"Not by much," she muttered and busied herself with Kitty this time.

"I do have drama queen tendencies," I said.

"Ha! You're the most laid-back person I've ever met. If you were any more laid-back you'd be in a coma."

"That's only because you're so uptight."

"I am not!" she screeched, standing in protest.

I laughed, making a point of sliding my gaze from her once occupied seat to her now indignant stance. "I think it's admirable. Honestly. I would love to get wound up about so many things."

"Oh, shut up!" She swiped my shoulder before huffing a bit more and dropping back into her seat. A long moment passed before she asked, "Do you know Molly? She works at some outfitter shop?"

"Yes." I felt my fingers cross behind my back hoping that Molly wasn't Lena's type. Then again, I didn't have any right to care if she were.

"Any reason you'd know of that she'd have my number and call to ask me out?"

My head shook and pulled back. What exactly was she asking me? "Like maybe I told her you were in need of a date? Is that what you're asking?"

She shrugged. "Maybe not desperate for a date but perhaps you encouraged her to call the new single lesbian in town?"

"I'd never do that. Your relationship status is not for me to advertise."

"I figured, but I asked Joanna and Brandy and they denied telling her anything."

That sounded right. Even if the ski instructors had told Molly, they probably wouldn't own up to it. They were a bit mischievous and liked starting things. One winter they handed out Vivian's business number as their own to all the women they'd bedded and now wanted to avoid. That was their idea of a joke, but poor Viv had to take calls from these hurt women for months. If she hadn't turned two of them into clients for her interior design business, she probably wouldn't have spoken to J&B again. Thankfully, as Christine's friend, they never messed with me. Christine could be very intimidating.

"Are you upset that some people know?"

"I just don't like being set up."

"No one does, or if they do, they're nuts." I thought for a moment, wondering if I should tell her that as soon as she told Terry, she'd told the whole town. I didn't want to bring up the board meeting that discussed terminating her contract. She didn't need to know that some people in town had the power to make her life hell.

"Definitely nuts," she agreed.

"Oh, wait," I said, trying to give Joanna and Brandy the benefit of the doubt. "You didn't happen to meet Camilla at Club Di, did you?"

"I met a lot of women that night."

"Short woman, long black hair, big mouth, but always smiling?"

Her eyes lifted to the left, contemplating. "She seems familiar."

"Tell her you're from Aspen?"

"Living here, yes."

"She's good friends with Molly and always looking out for new blood."

"Ah."

"One piece of advice?" I waited for her hesitant nod. "If you're not interested in dating Molly, you need to tell her. Otherwise she'll just think you're playing hard to get."

"Oh, jeez." She snuck a glance at me. "You've been there?"

"Her asking me out? Yes. Been with her? No. But she's a really nice lady. She can also wear you out on a mountain trail and will never get lost."

"As opposed to you," she shot. A second later her hand clamped over her mouth.

Before she could apologize for giving me a hard time about not being able to keep up on a hiking trail, I said, "I could have let you get lost, you know."

She smiled gratefully. "I appreciate that you didn't."

"You might find you have a lot in common with her."

"Not sure if dating in this town is a good idea. Joanna warned me against it. Kirsten, too." Her eyebrows rose in question as if I might give her insight.

"It is hard not to run into them at the supermarket."

Standing, she patted her leg to get the dogs moving. She nodded at me and stepped off the porch. "Guess it would be."

I might have been imagining it, but she sounded almost wistful when she agreed that it would be difficult to date someone in town.

From the Journal of Lena Coleridge:

Poor Mei. I feel for her. Six people have already asked if I'd heard about her separation. This town. Sometimes it feels like we're living in a box together. Can't be helping Mei any. Such a nice lady, too. Smart and funny, always happy to include me in their conversation whenever I find her at Glory's. She's lucky to have a friend like that. If anyone can help her through this tough time, upbeat, relaxed Glory is at the top of the list.

Speaking of which, I swear that woman almost flirted with me tonight. I'm bringing up my failed marriage and asking her about that woman she left with at the club, and suddenly, she comes dangerously close to flirting. If I know her, she's just trying to rile me up. Easy for her since nothing bugs her. She didn't even bat an eye when I asked if she'd pimped me out to Molly. Most people would get upset at the accusation, but not her. And Molly, talk about awkward. That phone call was no fun to return. "Yeah, hi, thanks for calling to ask me out sight unseen but just because we're both lesbians doesn't mean we're a match." Glory was right, though, better to tell her I'm not interested than string her along. Come to think of that, Mei isn't the only one lucky to have Glory as a friend. With or without the flirting.

Chapter 19

For the third time tonight, I felt like I was being stared at. I glanced around the restaurant, recognizing a lot of diners. No one seemed to be focused on me, but it was such a strange feeling.

"Something wrong?" Lena asked, taking a sip of wine.

"Must be left over from the tough day. Thanks again for letting me drag you out. I didn't feel like cooking tonight."

"I never feel like cooking."

I laughed, enjoying my new friend more and more. She was wonderfully cynical, but the best part was she didn't actually believe half the cynical stuff she said. It always made for an interesting evening.

"Am I too late to join you?" Mei asked, weaving toward our table.

Lena looked up, surprised but smiling. She pulled out the chair next to her. My heart lifted to see Mei out and acting like she used to. She'd done a few things with me, her parents, and Brooke, but otherwise, she stayed in or came over to my house. I couldn't blame her. People were still whispering whenever we walked by. The assumption was that Andy had dumped her, and most people felt sorry for Mei.

"Glad you're here," I told her and caught the waiter's attention so Mei could put in an order. "Today sucked for everyone in the office," I explained to Lena, not that she seemed to mind having a drop-in dinner guest.

"You were going to tell me about it, I think."

"Good luck with that." Mei nudged her. "She's not even bound by the courts not to talk about clients, but she's better at it than I am."

"My clients are less…" I searched for the right word.

"Guilty?" Mei inserted, causing Lena to snort on the sip of wine she took.

"I didn't know you did criminal defense work?" Lena asked her.

"Not usually. My clients get into all the other kind of trouble."

We laughed and settled into a nice conversation. Mei quirked her left eyebrow at me, something she'd perfected in high school to look intrigued. Without having to ask, I knew she was thinking how easy it was to chat with Lena. Very much like how she and I got on. So far, she'd managed to refrain from asking if I was developing feelings for Lena, which was a good thing. I wouldn't be able to answer that question yet. Whatever I felt for Lena couldn't be labeled yet.

Our food arrived just as a buzz started in the restaurant. I glanced up and caught Spencer walking up to the bar. No doubt he was grabbing a to-go order and heading home. Several diners called out greetings, forcing his eyes toward the tables. He said hello to some folks then saw us and smiled. He grabbed his to-go carton and came over.

"Friendly faces, just what I needed today." He squeezed my shoulder and touched Mei's before shaking Lena's hand.

"Join us," I offered, only slightly worried that Lena would be upset to have another person at the table. If she was going to be a good friend of mine, she'd better get used to it. I was the queen of changing plans to include others at the last minute.

"I couldn't," Spence hesitated.

"You're not going back to work," I insisted.

He seemed to be gauging whether or not to join us. Since Mei's separation, they hadn't been seen in public together. He made up his mind and took the seat next to me. "Maybe for a minute."

"Eat your dinner with us," Mei said, finally sounding like she wasn't letting her divorce bother her anymore.

Lena asked the waiter for a plate, apparently getting into the spirit of the community table. As tightly wound as she was, I was surprised that she didn't throw out some attitude at the change. She might be a little more laid-back than I gave her credit for.

"Hey, guys." Cassie greeted, walking up to the table with her sister-in-law, Vivian. They must have been dining on the other side of the giant fireplace out of view.

"Cass!" Spence smiled and stood to hug her. We'd all been in the same class in high school and remained close when we moved back.

"Viv, have you met Lena yet?" Cassie asked. She'd met Lena on my porch two weeks ago when she'd stopped by to pick up my contribution for her kids' soccer team. The ten minute expected visit turned into an hour long discussion on horses and dogs. They'd both walked off my porch that night with a new friend.

Vivian's golden brown tresses turned in Lena's direction, greenish-blue eyes passing over her. Approval glistened in the green-blue, adding another level of attractiveness to an already gorgeous package. And she was kind, too. So unfair. "Nice to meet you, Lena."

"And you, Vivian," Lena responded, taking the offered hand.

My mind was just processing the unwelcome realization that Vivian was closer to Lena's age when her eyes flicked to me. I felt my breath catch, recognizing the same look of approval she'd given Lena. Maybe she was just in a really good mood tonight. "Hi, Viv."

"Good to see you, Glory." She bent to buss my cheek then turned to do the same with Spence and Mei. Cassie was always trying to get her to come out with us, but she was often busy with work. We didn't see her as much as we'd like, but I understood concentrating on work.

They made their goodbyes, and their departure opened up the floodgates. Diners from all over the restaurant stopped by the table to shake the mayor's hand and officially meet Lena if they hadn't already. Many of them had a look of envy on their faces, almost like they wished they could join us. Spencer kept to his tight group of friends and family. As the mayor, he had to keep a wall up. I couldn't blame him, but I felt like he was missing out on some good friendships.

Once the tide of well wishers passed, we got back to enjoying dinner. Not surprisingly, Lena was able to hold her end of the conversation square. When she wasn't talking, she seemed to be studying us. Every once in a while I thought I caught a knowing smile creep onto her lips and a furtive glance at me. I couldn't interpret it, but it was nice to see.

By the time we were done, I was feeling worn out but much happier than when I'd left work. My clients had an exhaustive effect on me at times. Spending an evening with friends was a great way to erase that feeling.

Spence jumped into his car and offered Mei a ride to the house where she was staying. I hoped that they'd spend the evening together. In their plan to be seen as just friends, they hadn't spent a night together since Mei had left Andy. I didn't want their forced separation for the sake of appearances to back them off completely. A night reconnecting would do wonders for Mei.

Lena and I climbed into her car and headed toward our homes. It felt like we'd all been getting together for years, and it brought a smile to my lips.

"I'm sorry," she said.

I started forward, not knowing what she was apologizing for. I gave her a questioning look.

"For calling Spencer your beard."

"We already went through this."

"Yeah, but I didn't know that he was using you as his beard. I should have given you the benefit of the doubt."

I tilted my head, trying to think if anything happened at dinner that would have given her that impression. "What?"

"They've been together, what? Almost a year?"

"Who?" My heart thudded. Had I spilled the one secret I couldn't spill?

"You know who." She shot a knowledgeable look at me. "Was it your idea or Spencer's to start acting like you two were a couple?"

"We didn't act like we were a couple. I told you that."

"Right, yeah, I remember." She didn't sound convinced. "I've been curious about Mei's car in your driveway when I'd stop by and she wasn't around. Smart, really. How does she manage to get past Nancy's prying eyes?"

"Let's drop it."

Damn, she had guessed. From her house she wouldn't be able to see Mei's path from my driveway through the trees to Spencer's side gate. Not even Nancy had a view of that. That secluded path allowed them to keep their relationship secret from the beginning.

"You're right. It's none of my business." She turned onto our street and pulled into my driveway. "I won't say anything. I just wanted you to know that you're a good friend. To me, of course, but now I see just how good a friend you can be to others."

I absorbed that. "Thanks. Nice of you to say."

She grabbed my hand and squeezed. "I mean it. See you tomorrow?"

I smiled and got out of her car. My heart rate came back down. I could trust that she wouldn't say anything about Spencer and Mei. She was a good friend, too.

From the Journal of Lena Coleridge:

Okay, I know it's none of my business, but wow, Spencer and Mei? And Glory putting herself out there to help hide it. Like a mini soap opera in my own neighborhood. Not something I'd usually think is okay, but after seeing Mei with her husband at the fundraiser and now with Spence, it's so clear she belongs with Spence. Considering her husband was the one to start a lot of the gossip I've been hearing, I applaud Mei for getting out of that relationship. It's great to know that she will be able to move on and with a really nice guy.

Dinner was fun, even with the unexpected guests. The mayor has lots of admirers in town, and Mei and Glory seem to know everyone in town. I better get used to that if I'm going to keep hanging out with them. It does come with benefits. Glory has some really nice friends like Cassie, who stopped by the table tonight with her sister-in-law, Vivian. Gorgeous woman, that one. Family, too, that was easy to spot. Wonder if she's single. The way her eyes practically ate up Glory, I'll bet she is. Not that Glory noticed.

Can't quite figure that Glory out. She's either clueless or knows exactly what she wants. Both seem possible for someone so relaxed. Must be nice not to be constantly wondering what others think. I should take a lesson from her. Maybe after a few more months in this town, I'll get there.

Chapter 20

As weekends went, this one was going down as pretty mundane. I'd just gotten back from my parents' house where we'd watched a movie with Mei and her parents. Tomorrow, Mei and I would finish inventorying her assets for the divorce papers. It was the last formality on her part. I hoped that once she handed this to her attorney, Andy would stop dragging his heels and do his part. Either his disinterest was making this process more drawn out or he was regretting having let her slip out of his hands.

When the doorbell rang, I faced the door with a frown. Very few people would stop by this late other than Mei, Spence, or my parents, all of whom had keys and usually let themselves in.

"Hi," Lena greeted when I opened the door. She wore slacks and a halter top. The top showed off lots of smooth skin, which had recently darkened from beige to light sable in the summer sunshine. Once again, her wardrobe was sharp and tasteful. Not one misstep that I'd seen, even her casual jeans looked custom.

"What brings you by?"

Her arm lifted and a bag of empty containers dangled in my view. I smiled at the offering. It was so nice to have someone else to bake for now that my dad was on a strict diet. Client meetings always helped diminish my supply, but mostly, I'd end up freezing the leftovers and tossing them after months. Lena made for a guilt-free baking experience.

"Is this a hint for more?" I kidded, leading her back to my kitchen.

"Only if you feel up to it. I haven't had to stop by a bakery in ages. Should I be buying you flour, eggs, and sugar to encourage more?"

"You could help with the baking."

With a sly smile, she admitted, "You don't want that."

I did, actually. So much that the vision of us baking together in my kitchen distracted me.

"No one would want that," she continued, oblivious to my daydream of domesticity.

I shook myself to stop from wanting something I'd never wanted before. Talk about confusing. Could I really be thinking about sharing a life with someone? Just like that? One day I'm happy just to be alive, and the next it's not enough? Seems ungrateful, really.

"Where'd you go?" Lena's face was suddenly much closer, interest in her eyes.

Somewhere unmentionable, at least for now. "I was thinking I'd try something new tomorrow. How does pumpkin bread sound?"

Her head tilted, sweeping the hair that wasn't clipped back across one eye. "I've never heard of it, but that ginger cake was scrumptious and I'd never heard of that either." She tucked the hair behind her ear, leaving those beautiful brown eyes unobstructed. "That wasn't where you were, though."

Like she could know that. "Where do you think I went?"

"Somewhere serious and heavy. Places you don't like to go."

She couldn't know that either. "Yeah, I'm all surface all the time."

"I didn't say that. I said that you don't like to go there, most of us don't, but you, especially."

"Did I miss an M.D. in psychiatry on your résumé?"

She ignored the joke, her eyes slashing right through me. "Is it because you were forced to think about serious things from too young an age?"

I sat back against the barstool for balance. We were venturing into new territory. We'd sniped at each other before. I'd even been angry with her, something I rarely felt with anyone. Now she was asking questions that no one, not even my family, especially not my family had asked.

"You look so young, you are so young, but sometimes you act so, so—"

"Ancient, over the hill, out to pasture?" I joked to hide my discomfort.

"Then the jokes kick in and you're back to your teenage self."

"Have you seen my copy of *Twilight* around here?" I glanced around, biting back a grin. "Whenever she comes out with a new one, I have to read them all from the start again. I just love Edward. He's so dreamy."

"You're impossible." Lena shook her head, not as successful in holding back her smile as I'd been. "I can see that you don't like to talk about it. That's fine. I thought it might be easier to talk about with someone who wasn't here back then."

I considered that. It sounded nice. To be able to share how scared I'd been for much of my life. How much I hated that my parents had to go through any of it. How I couldn't allow myself to be negative. It wouldn't have helped anyone. On the contrary, it would have only served to scare everyone who cared about me more. Lena was right. I'd lived an entire lifetime by the time I was seventeen. That pretty much made me ancient now. Not that it made me any more willing to chat about it.

"Or maybe not," she muttered, backing up.

"Maybe you'd like to discuss why your sister's so worried about the singles' scene here?"

"Fair enough." Her lips curled. "Not exactly the same thing, but I take your point. If you ever feel the need to unburden yourself, I am good for more than a rundown of the day's events over a beer on the porch."

I gave a slight nod. "I'll keep that in mind."

She grasped my forearm and squeezed, sliding her hand down to mine. Awareness raced through me. Her hand was soft and warm. My perpetually cold hand clutched hers instinctively, seeking that warmth. Or that's how my mind justified clinging to her hand. It felt so good in mine.

Her eyes dropped to our hands before rising to meet mine again. Something raw sparkled there. She turned away, taking her hand with her. I wanted it back, missing and craving her touch, an unfamiliar sensation, unacceptable as well. This wasn't good. Attraction was one thing; genuine feelings were something entirely different.

"I should head home." She took a step toward the front door.

"Thanks for returning the containers." It seemed like the best response given my alternatives: *Will you please have hot, lusty sex with me? What the hell do you put in your hair to make it so damn shiny and perfect? Whatever it is makes me want to have hot, lusty sex with you. Also stop figuring me out because it's getting to the point where I'm going to have to kill you for knowing so much. It's an annoying trait that makes me want to have hot, lusty sexy with you. I'm not normally annoyed, and I've never had hot, lusty sex. Mild, healthy sex, but not hot or lusty, and you make me want to have it.* As her neighbor and friend, I think I chose my response wisely. No need to ruin a good friendship and bring on awkwardness in the neighborhood.

Lena hesitated. For a moment it seemed like she was able to hear my inner dialogue, or perhaps she was having one of her own. She turned back, coming closer.

In the next instant, I found myself in her arms. An infinitely better feeling than holding her hand.

Too soon, the hug ended and Lena was walking backward. "Goodnight, Glory."

I watched her stumble on the edge of a chair before she turned and double-timed it to the door. I was glad to see I wasn't the only one affected tonight.

From the Journal of Lena Coleridge:

I hugged her! I shouldn't have done that. She felt so good. I knew she was going to feel that good. I hate being right.

She's my neighbor. She's practically a baby even if she acts like she's an old soul. I shouldn't have tried to get her to open up about her heart surgery in high school. How could discussing something that happened so long ago push us into dangerous territory? It couldn't, but I'm glad she shut it down. There's no telling how I would have reacted if she'd opened up. Screw hugging her, I might have kissed her. Might have jumped her even, which would be a huge mistake. Neighbor. Young. Guarded. Neighbor. Not to mention how infuriating she is with her laid-back, nothing bothers me, let me see if I can get under your skin, attitude.

Bad arms, with the hugging. Bad, bad arms.

Chapter 21

Leaning over the pool table, I lined up what I hoped would be the final shot of this match. Cassie and I were partnered up for a charity tournament to prevent animal cruelty. The farther we went in the tournament, the more money we raised from our sponsors. I made a good teammate, less so for my pool skills than for my wealthy client list.

"Good shot." Cassie knocked my knuckles after I'd sunk the eight ball for the win.

"Eiben!" Mitch growled as he stared down at the last pocket, his dreams of winning the tournament now gone.

Cassie rolled her eyes at his constant use of everyone's last names. Then she punched his arm to break him out of the despair.

"Yeats!" Mitch growled at her, rubbing his huge bicep.

Andy, his pool partner, laughed and shook our hands. He didn't like losing any more than Mitch did, but he was better at hiding his annoyance. Neither was too upset to accept a sloppy kiss from one of my least favorite former schoolmates Abby. She kissed both men, despite Mitch being married and Andy in the middle of a divorce. She had been Andy's girlfriend before he started dating Mei. She hadn't taken that well, and Mei had suffered her bad attitude ever since.

Abby continued to cling to Andy, giving off a territorial signal. Everyone nearby seemed as surprised as I was by the affectionate display. It didn't mesh with the town gossip that Andy and Mei were both upset by the divorce. He sure didn't look concerned when he accepted another kiss from the clearly tipsy Abby. I wasn't looking forward to telling Mei that her soon to be ex-husband seemed to enjoy flaunting his newly single status, but I couldn't let her be blindsided either.

"I'm going to grab some air," I told Cassie, not enjoying the show Abby was putting on.

I waved at Vivian and Molly on the way out. They were our next opponents. Molly was good; Vivian not as much, but like me, Viv had a great client list to help Cassie raise money. If we beat them, we'd face Spencer and his buddy James. We didn't have a hope of winning that one. James had his own pool table and could clear a table in one turn.

"Home wrecker."

I turned in the direction of the inebriated accuser, curious to see if it was a local or a tourist getting the dressing down. Abby was walking through the front door, following me. I twisted to see if she was talking to someone else, but we were the only two people outside. "Excuse me?"

"You heard me. It's one thing to break up a marriage, but it's another to pervert someone to your ways."

Giving her my full attention, I reversed my course to close the distance between us. "What are you talking about?"

"Don't act all innocent." She swiped at her too blond curls to push them out of her face. In her inebriated state, she forgot about the copious amount of hairspray she used. Her fingers snagged halfway through. "Andy told me about you. Not that he cares that his wife left him, but leaving him for you, especially since you're supposed to be his friend is tearing him up inside."

"Are you injured? Maybe on your head somewhere?" I asked her. She was accusing me of luring Mei away from Andy? What the hell?

"I'm just drunk enough to finally speak my mind. You and Mei make me sick. You've probably been secretly screwing behind Andy's back for years."

I wanted to walk away. Normally I would have, but this was such an outrageous accusation that I just couldn't. I'd never told Abby I was gay. In order to preserve some privacy in a small town, I'd only told my close friends. Abby wasn't on that list. "You honestly believe that Mei and I are romantically involved and were prior to her separation?"

"Don't act like you aren't some big dyke. I was fooled, everyone in town was fooled, but Andy let me know about you. It doesn't take a genius to figure out that Mei left him for you. What's almost as bad is that you're hurting our mayor in the process. What do you think Spence would do if he knew his girlfriend was a dyke? Maybe I should tell him."

Oh, for heaven's sake. "Abby, you're drunk. Get a cab and sleep it off." I turned to head back into the bar.

"Don't ignore me." She tried to grab my arm but missed and stumbled.

I faced her to prevent her from injuring herself. "Mei did not leave Andy for me. That's ridiculous. I know Andy doesn't believe that. You should spend your energy wrapping him up instead of spreading lies."

"Oh, I'll get him. Had I been more experienced in high school I never would have lost him, but he's mine now." Her brown eyes blazed like I was going to make a move on him. "I'm just making sure that you and Mei get what's coming to you."

I tried for calm. "Divorce is hard enough. Let them work through it."

"What about Spencer?"

"What about him, Abby? I'm not his girlfriend. We're just friends. That's all we've ever been,"

Confusion knitted her brow. "But you're a lesbo."

"Ahh, drunk Abby, we've missed you so," Cassie crooned as she stepped outside into our conversation circle.

"Bite me, Cass," Abby retorted then looked at me. "That's probably something you'd like." Her smile was smug, thinking she'd spilled a state secret to one of my friends.

"Biting's always fun," Cassie declared, looping an arm around me.

"What? You know?" Abby's brow was getting a wrinkle workout.

"Know what?" Cassie looked at me for clarification.

"My sexual preference. Abby's giving a news report."

Cassie laughed. "Get a life, Abby, and mind your own business."

"I can't believe you knew." Abby looked devastated. "I thought you were Andy's friend. How could you just stand by and watch her seduce his wife?"

Cassie doubled over with laughter this time. "Seriously? Glory seducing Mei? That's nuts, Abs. Whoever told you that is crazy."

Abby looked even more confused. I should be thanking Cassie for getting through to her. Mei didn't need the headache and heartache of having rumors flying around about her marriage. Divorce was hard enough without rumors. "But why would Mei leave Andy?"

"That's none of your business either. You need to sleep this off, okay? Let's get Patsy to give you a ride home." Cassie steered Abby toward the entrance. She glanced back at me and winked, knowing she'd diffused the situation. I felt a sigh of relief slip through my lips. Mei owed Cassie a fruit basket or something.

* * *

Brooke poked her head into my office after she'd walked her clients out. She wore a bright smile but looked a bit tired. I checked my watch. She'd already been here nine hours.

"Want to tell me why those were the third clients to ask me if the rumors about you being gay were true?"

"Oh, gaawwd. Really?"

"I'm pretty sure it's why some of them made appointments with me today."

"This town." I rolled my eyes.

"Tell me about it." She dropped heavily into a chair. "Who's talking?"

I recalled drunk Abby. "Andy probably. Seems he can't keep his mouth shut about anything these days."

She nodded, shoulders slumping. "No kidding. He cornered me in the grocery store the other day. He doesn't seem to be too sad over the divorce, but he sure as hell seemed concerned that Mei shouldn't be having any fun."

"Men, huh?"

She smiled and glanced at her wedding ring. "Sometimes I wonder if I've got the only good one."

"He is pretty good."

Brooke's husband, David, was great, actually. Besides the wonderful personality, he was a master handyman who'd saved our business bank account with all the repairs to this house. Hundred year old homes were maintenance nightmares.

"If you'd settle down with someone, no one would be whispering around town." She brushed an unworried hand through the air. "Once you're a couple, you're old, boring news."

"That easy, huh?" I joked.

"I hear your neighbor might be a candidate."

"Now who's gossiping? Did Mei say something?" Heat flared straight to my cheeks.

She sat up straighter, eyes twinkling. "No, Jennifer told me about Lena. Why? What does Mei know? I wasn't just making a wild guess?"

"Very wild."

Her eyebrows shot up. "I've met her a few times in passing. She seems lovely."

"Don't you start."

"Someone else has already started?" She gave me a wicked smile. "Mei? Your parents?"

"Both, and I don't want to hear it from you, thanks."

"Dinner party at my house," she declared. "I'll invite the usual suspects and you can invite Lena."

"It's your party."

"Baby," she accused and stood up. "Fine. I'll invite her. This is going to be fun."

She delivered on her promise. All of Brooke's dinner parties were fun, but this one was especially entertaining. She and David played wonderful hosts. Hazel and her husband added to the comical atmosphere. Mei and Spencer finally seemed relaxed again. Brooke's neighbors on both sides of her house joined us last, and everyone helped make Lena feel welcome.

"Were you a high school principal back in Baltimore, Lena?" Brooke's neighbor Julie asked.

"Yes, and middle school before that."

"Did you go for the hat trick with elementary?" Julie's husband joked.

Lena made a face. "No thanks. You spend more time talking to parents than dealing with kids in elementary school."

"You must like kids," Brooke's other neighbor Leo said.

"Short humans make life interesting," she agreed.

"They sure do." Spencer wrapped an arm around me, and everyone laughed. He towered over me by close to a foot. Even Brooke's daughter grew taller than me last year.

"But she's been out of high school at least three years, hasn't she?" Lena joked, shooting me a teasing glare.

"I remember when she came to work for me after college," Brooke started, "I swear she looked younger than when she left for school. This one, too." She pointed at Mei.

"Is there a portrait of you both somewhere?" Spence teased. He had no room to talk. If he'd shave that beard, he'd look younger than we did.

"Visited a crossroads while you were in college?" Hazel's husband offered.

"Such faith you have in us," Mei said.

"Notice she didn't deny it." David elbowed Leo. He often kidded his wife about trying to keep up with her decade plus younger partners. It was a running joke because Brooke was more active than either of us.

I glanced at my watch, shocked that it was already so late. "I hate to be the one to shut down the fun, but I've got an early appointment and Brooke has to wake with the roosters."

Everyone took their time saying goodbye and heading out. Spencer, Mei, Lena and I piled into his car and headed back home. It was like we'd been doing this hundreds of times. The three of us had, but adding Lena to the mix hadn't changed the dynamic. A blessing really, considering how much I liked Lena.

Chapter 22

Spending Saturday doing yard work would have been so much less fun without Ashlyn's help. She mowed lawns for a lot of her neighbors, but I'd get her over here a few times a year to do some major pruning and planting. We'd been at it an hour, and I felt completely wiped out. Perhaps it was the heat, but I couldn't keep going without a break.

"Need some lemonade?"

Ashlyn looked up, wiping her arm across her brow. It left a dirt streak on her shiny forehead. She'd been working really hard, much harder than I had. If I weren't so tired, I'd feel guilty.

I collapsed into a chair on the porch and reached into the cooler. Ashlyn bolted up the steps with more energy than I'd ever had, joining me in the other chair. She grabbed the bottle and took in half the lemonade in one drink, wiping her mouth with the back of her hand.

When she noticed me watching her, she smiled sheepishly. "Sorry. Mom says I need to work on my manners."

I shrugged. "I'm the one that's been making you work for an hour in the hot sun without offering you anything to drink. Make sure to help yourself for the rest of the day."

"Okay."

"Are you going to volleyball camp again this summer?"

"I don't think so." She looked away.

Without needing to press, I knew it was because her parents wouldn't pay for it. Sometimes I wanted to shake them and make them notice how great a kid they had. When other teenagers would be giving attitude and causing trouble, Ashlyn ran her own business, excelled at sports, and got amazing grades.

"Junior year is when scouts start getting serious, right?" I tried not to sound like I was pressuring her, but her coach wouldn't be able to do it. He wasn't so much a volleyball coach as an English teacher who needed the extra income.

"I think so."

"Those camps would make a big difference in getting you on their radar."

"Yeah, probably." She tried not to look defeated, but I could tell she was really disappointed.

"I like that you're a modest kid, Ash, but you're in the best position to know if you have a shot at a scholarship. You're playing against kids all over the state and last year's camp was in California. You saw the best athletes there. How do you think you measured up?"

Her cheeks went pink and she looked away. Modest was right. "I did okay."

"You got to choose teams every time, I bet." If she'd been a team captain, she was definitely one of the best in the camp.

She shrugged, acknowledging my guess. "Almost every time."

"You should be getting letters this fall, but I bet there'd be a lot more if you went to that camp, right?"

"Probably."

I let that hang in the air for a while. "It might be time for you to decide what's more important. Having enough money saved up in case you have to pay for college, or spending some of that money for a better chance at a scholarship."

I knew I was crossing a boundary that a non-family member shouldn't cross, but her parents were so overwhelmed by the triplets they let too many things slide with her. I took care of their finances and taxes. It wasn't too much of a leap to include Ashlyn's financial situation in that mix.

"It isn't just spending the money."

"It isn't?"

"Not really. I wouldn't be making any money for those three weeks either. And I couldn't help with the Trips or Kyle."

I considered that, holding my tongue about how the Trips and her brother weren't her responsibility. "Have you asked your parents?"

"No."

"If you could make what you'd make over those three weeks before you leave, would that make a difference?"

She giggled. "I can't mow people's lawns more than once a week, Glor."

"No, but Spence asked me to talk to you today about some extra yard work. The Vic needs the conference room and kitchen painted. I want to put down a floor in my garage, hang some storage, and paint the guest room. And my parents are in desperate need of some closet and cabinet organization."

Her eyes grew wide as the possibilities came into view. "Really?"

"Spence wants you to start as soon as you can. You'll make more than you would mowing lawns for three weeks. My parents would probably buy you a car if you could make it so they can find things in their closets."

She giggled again. It was a fun sound. The kind of sound all teenage girls should make on a regular basis. "I'll talk to my parents."

"Sounds like the right move to me." I glanced over and noticed that the troubled look she brought here this morning wasn't completely gone. "What else is up?"

She drank down the rest of her lemonade and stood. "Not much. Better get back to it."

I stood with her but had to reach out to grab her shoulder for balance. The rush nearly made me topple back into my chair. That hadn't happened in a long time. I didn't think I'd been working that hard. Gardening was the best type of exercise for me. It used nearly every muscle without being aerobic.

"You okay, Glory?" Ashlyn now had both hands on my arms. She looked panicked by my unsteady stance.

"Yeah, thanks. It's a lot hotter than I thought. Must be dehydrated."

"Sit. Let me work. That's what you're paying me for, right?" She forced a laugh, still worried. The last thing she'd want to deal with today would be having her mentor keel over in front of her.

"I'm good. We'll take some water bottles with us this time." I took a small step, testing my balance. It came back, but I still felt tired. More than I'd been over the past two weeks when I'd find myself taking longer to do almost everything. It was moments like this, though, that made me realize something might be wrong. It could be the heat and exertion, but I'd have to monitor my status until I was sure it wasn't anything else.

"Sure, okay." Ashlyn reached into the cooler and took out two bottles of water. She shadowed my every step back out into the front yard. If I looked back, I'd probably see her arms outstretched ready to catch me if I fell.

We both settled back onto the knee pads and picked up where we'd left off. I was weeding and she was reshaping plants. We had bark to spread later and a few tree branches that needed tending. If my energy didn't perk up, we might have to stretch that out over the next couple of days.

"You were going to tell me what else was up?" I urged again. Sometimes it took a few nudges before Ash opened up.

"You won't say anything?"

This was always a tricky one. "If it's something I think your parents should know, I'll encourage you to tell them. Strongly."

"It's nothing like that. You know my friend Maddy?" She waited until I nodded, recalling that Maddy had come to the office a few times with Ashlyn and Brooke's daughter, Izzy. They were all on the volleyball team together. "She, um, she told me she was gay."

I kept my face blank, hoping to get everything from her before I said anything. I tilted my head, encouraging her to continue.

"She's afraid to tell her parents. She's been stressing for weeks. I don't know how to help her. I just feel bad." The tightness in her shoulders had eased, clearly relieved to get this off her chest.

"Are her parents the type to freak over news like this?" I'd met them a few times whenever Brooke had them over for dinner parties. They seemed very nice, but no one could predict how a parent might respond to this kind of news.

She shrugged. "She gets along great with them, but who knows? They're always asking if she has a boyfriend or which boy she likes. I think it'll be a surprise, but it's not like I think they'll kick her out or anything."

I let out a breath I didn't realize I'd been holding. Poor kid. I never had to go through that. My instincts told me that my parents wouldn't be fazed. I probably should have been nervous, but I was completely secure in how much they loved and accepted me. "Has she ever had a boyfriend?"

"No way. She's never been interested in boys."

"So you always knew?"

She contemplated that. "Pretty much. I didn't really think about it, like label it or anything, but I'm glad she told me."

"Was she nervous telling you?"

"Yep. Never seen her that way before."

"Could that be how she's thinking of her parents? Maybe worried for nothing?"

Ashlyn's eyes blinked, her head tilting up to look at the sky. "Do you think? Like maybe they know already?"

"Possibly. It may be why they're always asking her about a boyfriend. Give her the opportunity to tell them."

"God, that would be great. She's so stressed."

"Does she know there are support lines she can call?"

Her head was nodding. "Yeah, we got some brochures from the guidance counselor's office. She may call. I'm just trying to keep her calm."

"You're a good friend, Ash. A big support for her."

"Thanks."

"If she needs an adult to talk to, I'd be happy to talk with her." That might be crossing a more precarious boundary since I didn't have a connection to Maddy, but I had to make the offer.

"Yeah?" She glanced up, pausing with the clippers. She carefully put them down and picked up the branch cutters. "Because you're gay, too, right?"

My eyebrows rose. I couldn't tell if she was guessing or if someone had told her. She and I had a mentor-student thing going. As such, it was my job to listen and guide not focus on me. I would have told her had she asked, but she never had until now. "Yes, but that's not the only reason I'd talk to her. Sometimes you just need to hear from someone other than your best friend that everything has a way of working out eventually. It might be a tough road to get there, but it will happen."

"Thanks, Glory. That's cool. I'll let her know."

"Anything else on your mind or did we cover it?"

She giggled again. "Nope. Think we got to everything." She gave me a grateful smile and headed toward my garage. "I'll get the ladder. We can start on the trees next."

She really had matured over the past year. I was looking forward to her graduating college so I could grab her up as a trusted friend.

Chapter 23

Before I turned onto my street, I caught sight of Lena's dogs up ahead. I slowed the car because they were being walked by an elderly couple who were stopped at the intersection, looking down the road in every direction. When they heard my car approaching, the woman waved me to a stop.

I rolled down my window and accepted the doggie snouts that shoved inside for my attention. The couple tried pulling them back, but they were pretty excited to see me. "Hello. Are you just starting your stroll or are you on your way back to Lena's?"

"On our way back," the man said. He was probably in his eighties, tall and slim, African American, handsome with a full head of grey curly hair.

"Trying," the woman clarified. She looked younger than the man, Asian, short and slender, beautiful with more black than grey chin length hair. "We have been up and down this block ten times."

"We have not, my darling," the man corrected gently.

"I'm going to ride this dog home if we don't figure out which street we need." She pointed at an enthusiastic Kitty. "Are we even close?"

I laughed with the man and gauged how close a half mile would be for an elderly couple. "Why don't you jump in and I'll give you a ride back. It's still a ways to go. I'm Glory by the way. Lena's neighbor."

"That would be wonderful, but the dogs," the woman said.

"No problem. They've been in my car and house many times before."

"They do seem to like you," the man told me, pulling on Kitty's leash to get him to jump down. "If you're sure you don't mind. I'm Owen and this is my wife, Tamiko."

I got out and opened the back hatch to let the dogs jump into my car. Owen opened the back door for his wife and settled into the front seat when I got behind the wheel. Pulling back onto the street, I got us headed toward home.

"I told you we'd passed the street we needed, Owen."

"You're right, my darling; you always are." He shot me a wink before glancing at Nancy and Calvin's house.

"The architect who built this place also built three others on the street you were just on. It's easy to get turned around."

In no time, we were pulling into Lena's driveway. Her door opened at the sound. She came toward us as we got out of the car and I went to free the dogs. "Did you run out of gas?" she asked Tamiko as they embraced.

Side by side, it was easy to spot the resemblance. Lena's eyes were a shade lighter but otherwise identical in shape and positioning. They shared the same cheekbone structure, too. I'd probably spot all the similarities if I wanted to be rude and stare for longer. With Owen, too.

"You weren't kidding about the altitude," Owen told her.

"We should have tied a string to us before we left," Tamiko said.

"Ahh," Lena laughed, taking the leashes from me. "You found them where?"

"Only a half street off course. They would have found it eventually." I nodded in assurance to the man I assumed was her grandfather.

"Ha!" Tamiko declared, not giving her husband a way out. "We would have been walking for days if not for our rescuer. Thank you, dear."

"You're welcome, Tamiko. Owen, nice meeting you."

"Thank you, Glory. I'll never live this down, but I'm happy that my knees won't be sore tomorrow."

Lena's smile sparkled at me. "Shouldn't I be surprised that you've already met my grandparents on the first day of their visit?"

"Nope, small town and even smaller neighborhood."

Her grin widened as she studied me. "How about dinner with us on Saturday? Erica and her family will be out from Maryland by then."

I made an effort at polite. "I don't want to crash your family reunion."

"You won't be, dear," Tamiko told me before Lena could.

"It'll be fun to have fresh blood at the table," Owen inserted.

I laughed. "Sure, sounds good."

* * *

When I brought in my plate from Lena's deck, she was the only one in the kitchen. Erica and her eldest daughter had been in there just moments before, but it looked like they abandoned Lena to the dishes.

"Dinner was delicious," I said, scraping the food scraps into the trash.

"Papa is the barbeque master. Eri's husband thinks he's good, but Papa can put him to shame."

"Competition seems to be a thing with your family."

She laughed and bumped against me before handing me a towel when I offered help. "Competition is the only thing in our family."

"Your grandparents are great."

She turned to face me with a warm smile. "They are my heroes. Aside from being great people, their families both turned them away when they fell in love. They were able to repair the connection, but it took a long time before my grandma's traditional Japanese family came around to the idea of a black son-in-law. His family wasn't much more accepting."

"They're your mom's parents?"

"Yes."

"Your grandma is very beautiful. Is your mom as much of a looker?"

"I think she is. Eri takes after Grandma. I'm more of a combo of both grandmothers."

"I see your grandma's eyes and cheekbones, but I also see your grandfather's ears, chin, and long fingers." I glanced into her living room. "If you show me photos of your other grandparents I bet I can Mr. Potato Head the rest of your face."

She laughed again. "You know what I like about you?"

"My porch and free beverages?" I joked to hide the flush that ran through me at her words.

"Those, too," she agreed with a chuckle. "But it's how accepting you seem to be. You didn't even blink when I told you they were my grandparents."

"Why would I, even if I hadn't guessed?"

"Most of my friends who've met them think I'm kidding or toss out some racist question about why my features aren't more black or Japanese."

"These are friends of yours?" My eyebrows rose automatically.

She shrugged as if it she'd let it go a long time ago. The tiny braids in her hair jiggled at the movement. Of the hairstyles I'd seen, this was the most involved. It must have taken hours to pleat the long strands into what looked like millions of braids.

I felt myself blush when she caught me staring at the mesmerizing style. "I have to say that hair is pure genius."

"Thank you," Erika's daughter said as she came into the kitchen again. "My sister and I did it last night. We could do yours." Her hands were already reaching for my hair. "Ooh, feel this, Aunt Lena. So soft, like a baby's hair. Mom! Come feel."

Lena's mouth nudged ajar as she watched her niece's fingers scrunch chunks of my hair. "Taylor!"

Erika stopped in the doorway at the scene. "Tay, leave the nice lady's hair alone."

"I can't; it's so soft." Her dazed voice made us laugh.

I didn't need to touch hers to know that her curly mass would be thick and sturdy. "Not sure my hair could withstand tight braids, kid."

Her hands dropped away. "Definitely not."

I rejoined Lena at the sink to finish up the dishes. Her eyes kept drifting back to my hair as her niece suggested styles for my hair type. She looked like she wanted to test the softness for herself. I found myself wishing she would.

All night she'd been almost bubbly. It was clear how happy she was to be surrounded by family. She'd told me after Erika's first visit how much she missed being able to get together with them on weekends. I was glad to see that this experience wasn't making her wistful.

"What's going on in here?" Tamiko demanded, stepping up beside Erika. "Are you making your guest do dishes, Lena? Didn't I teach you better?"

"Yeah, Ms. No Manners," Erica taunted.

"She offered, Ms. Free Loading Visitor who has yet to cook or clean in all the time she's stayed here."

"Girls!" Tamiko scolded.

Instead of being horrified by the scolding, they burst into laugher. It was easy to imagine Tamiko taking care of them when they were younger. I felt the warmth and caring they had for each other. Usually I'd see something like this and feel sad that I didn't have siblings to spar with, but tonight it was satisfying enough to be near it.

Lena was becoming more and more important in my life. It made me happy to see that her family seemed supportive of her move here. It meant she would likely stick around. Seeing as I was rapidly becoming dependant on seeing her regularly, I was almost as happy as she was about the support.

Chapter 24

One last patch of ivory remained in my guest bedroom. Ashlyn attacked it as well as she'd covered the rest of the room. I'd finished with the edging a few minutes before and stood back to take in the sage green color. It would go really well with the new bedspread I'd bought. My mom would love the color of her assigned room the next time she stayed over.

"I'll put the ladder back," Ashlyn said, packing it up and hauling it away.

I followed her out of the room, veering off to the kitchen with the brush and roller. My arm ached, but I was glad to finish the room. It was one of those projects that had been nagging at me since I'd had the house built.

"Look who I found?" Ashlyn called out when she came back from the garage.

I looked up from the kitchen sink to see Lena being dragged into view. "Hey, neighbor, how's your day?"

"Good. Been painting?" She eyed the paint stains on our arms and faces.

"Want to see, Ms. Coleridge? We just finished the guest room." Ashlyn was already pulling her down the back hallway.

Rinsing out the last brush, I set the painting tools aside to dry. I could hear Ashlyn describing the process and paint color choice. It had gone much better than when I'd helped Christine. Probably because no one had to face a hormone crazed pregnant woman if we didn't get it right.

They both joined me in the kitchen after the tour. "Looks really great," Lena commented.

"All thanks to Ash."

"No," she denied modestly. "We did it together."

"Either way, it looks wonderful. I know who to call when I get around to changing colors in my house."

Ashlyn blushed, obviously overjoyed by the attention and compliments. I was increasingly impressed by this girl. I wouldn't have been able to have a regular conversation with my principal outside of school when I was a junior.

"Thanks, Glory. I'll start on the garage floor Monday," she said, accepting the check I handed her. "I better get home and help with dinner. Bye, Ms. Coleridge. Hope you're having a nice summer."

"I am, Ashlyn, thanks. See you soon."

We watched her bound out of the house and laughed at the same time. "Energy," Lena said.

"Endless energy."

She looked relaxed in her capris and scoop neck shirt. The braids were gone now, back to loose and natural. She'd been in Denver for the last few days, showing her grandparents around before putting them on a plane. "I wanted to see if you were free for dinner."

I was, and really wanted to go, but I was also really tired. "Do you mind if we just stay here?"

She stepped forward, concern showing on her face. "Did she run you into the ground?"

"My arm feels like it's going to fall off." My legs and back, too, but I didn't want to sound like a wimp. I hadn't felt this tired after painting Christine's room, but maybe I'd been overexerting myself lately.

"Dinner here sounds good. Want me to go pick something up?"

"That would be great. It'll give me a chance to shower some of this paint off." I pointed to the three visible patches on my arms and neck. "Whatever you're in the mood for is fine with me."

Her glance turned serious for a moment. She looked like she was trying to find something to say but gave up, nodded, and headed out without another word. If I had more energy, I'd wonder what just went through her mind. As it was, I'd be lucky to make it to the shower.

The water and soap woke me up, cleaning and energizing all at once. My farmer's tan seemed to make the rest of my skin look ghost-like in the mirror when I stepped out to dry off. I would have to make time to sit out in the privacy of my backyard soon for a little more consistent coverage. Only the reddish pink of my surgery scar added any color to my torso. The thick, jagged line ran from center sternum to a couple inches above my belly button. Ugly thing, really ugly, even to someone who tried to stay positive, but it was the reason I was alive.

I ran my fingers over the rough, raised scar. It was actually a series of six scars, one on top of the other. The close study brought on a reminder that I'd been feeling more tired than usual lately. I brushed off the thought, chalking it up to the increased activities over the past couple of weeks.

The doorbell rang as I was slipping on a camisole. A second later, I heard Lena call out that she was back and letting herself in. I smiled at my reflection, trying not to examine why her announcement made me so happy. I really liked her and the fact that she was my neighbor was becoming less of an issue for me. I hadn't tried to have a real relationship since leaving college, and I'd never attempted one in this too small town. I couldn't help feeling this would be a stupid move if we moved past friendship. Especially stupid if she didn't feel the same way.

Dressed but leaving my hair wet, I headed out into the dining room. Lena had set plates and put out the salads and sandwiches she'd picked up. She was just setting down the water pitcher when she looked up. Her eyes looked over and scanned me from head to toe. When they skated back up slowly, I thought perhaps I wasn't the only one fighting an attraction to her neighbor.

"Hey," Lena said and cleared her throat. "I made myself at home. Hope you don't mind."

"Not at all. Looks delicious."

"We're not in a hurry if you want to dry your hair." Her fingers gestured to my wet hair. For a second I thought they might brush against my head, but she pulled them back before making contact.

"I'll air dry tonight. I'm starving. Thanks so much for running to get dinner. I don't think I could have waited to make something."

She laughed as we both took our seats. "What would you have done if I hadn't come by?"

"Popcorn and lemonade." I started eating, thankful that I didn't have to resort to my plan.

"Come on." Even her doubtful expression looked beautiful.

"Serious. Check the cupboards. I've got boxes of microwave popcorn as my fallback."

"Iron stomach of youth, huh?"

"You're pretty hung up on age, aren't you?"

She took a bite of her sandwich, stalling. "Just yours."

"Because?" I wasn't going to let her off the hook. It seemed like we'd been close to flirting many nights, but we never trudged through set boundaries.

She mixed the dressing into her salad before responding. "My ex was five years younger and acted like a child most of the time."

That was a good reason to be hung up on age, all right. "You didn't clue in to that before you committed to her?"

"Stop," she responded to my kid by pushing against my shoulder and snorting. "You know how it is. You always put your best self forward at first. That goes away as you become more trusting of the relationship, but she managed to keep it up until right after we'd gone through the commitment ceremony."

"Sucks."

"Yep. I still can't believe I was fooled for more than a year. Who can keep up a front for that long?"

Really sucks. "Your ex?"

She laughed at my guess and looked relieved by it. "I felt like I was taking care of an entitled adolescent rather than sharing a life with a partner. It didn't take long to figure out that she'd married me for my money. I tried to work things out with her, but she lost interest when I followed my therapist's advice and closed down the Bank of Lena."

Bank of Lena? That must have stung. "I'm sorry."

She let out a long breath. "I'm not. It was a big mistake from the start."

"When did it end?"

"About a year now."

"Still fresh, then."

She tilted her head and examined me. "Not so much anymore."

I couldn't help but smile. That felt very personal. "But the age thing is a trigger?"

"It is when I'm standing on the edge of the same cliff."

Her words settled over us. The quiet seemed to rise to an uproar. I was pretty sure she'd just admitted to at least considering a relationship with us. If I was being honest, I'd been thinking the same thing since the start of summer. It was getting harder and harder to keep from touching her when we sat out on the porch together.

"You're saying what exactly?"

Her brown eyes bounced up to search mine. I hoped my tone conveyed that she wasn't the only one at the edge of the cliff. "That I've been wanting to rip your clothes off for weeks now."

I felt my breath leave me. My heart began to pound and it was all I could do to stay focused. "I would say you should buy me dinner first, but you already have." My joke broke through the tension, my stomach untwisting and her shoulders relaxing.

"Yeah, so." She shrugged, not sure where to go.

I cleared the dishes, taking some time to think. "You're not the only one."

She looked up from setting her glass in the sink. She nodded and thought for a moment. "The smart thing would be to stay as we are."

I smiled, happy that I wasn't the only one fighting being prudent. "That would be the smart thing."

She turned back from the sink. Her gaze seared into mine, and I felt a current run through my body. Everything we'd just talked about flushed out of my mind. In that moment, my only focus was her.

I stepped toward her and that was enough. She pulled me against her and her mouth took mine. There was no other way to describe the kiss. She took everything I had to give. The feel of her mouth overwhelmed and excited. I'd never been kissed like this before. Never understood the power of a kiss until her. I could stop with this if I had to. That had never happened before. Kisses didn't do this to me, but it was that satisfying.

Lena had other ideas, though. Her hands started roaming, touching my back, neck, arms, and stomach. They felt almost as good as her mouth. One hand shot under my shirt then stopped. She pulled her mouth away and asked, "A camisole? In this heat?"

It had been hot today, but I always ran on the cool side. Plus it covered my scar when I wore v-necks. It was difficult to form a response when she'd blasted my mind clear of all thoughts but the kissing. The amazing, excellent, superb, unequaled kissing.

"Weren't you talking about clothes earlier?"

"Taking them off, yes. Let's get to that." She stole another kiss then pushed us into motion.

As I led her to my bedroom, I no longer cared that this wasn't a smart move for us. I couldn't allow myself to think that if it didn't work out, we'd be in an awkward living situation until one of us moved. All I wanted was to feel her against me.

Nerves assaulted me when I opened the bedroom door, but Lena didn't let them settle. She tilted to slant her mouth against mine, chasing away all doubts. Soft yet demanding, her lips pulled pleasure through me. Her tongue darted along the seam of my lips, teasing until I opened to allow her inside. Fire blazed at the touch of her tongue against mine.

More, I needed more. I reached to unbutton her shirt, pulling it off in seconds. Her pants came next, pooling at her sandals. She stepped out of them as her hands got rid of my shorts. I broke away just long enough to pull off my shirt.

She pushed me onto the bed. I slid back, studying every inch of her. Tiny red dots jumped out on her black bra and matching panties. My mouth went dry at the sight of all that silky skin just waiting for my touch. Sexy as hell.

The bed dipped as she crawled up toward me. I felt myself thrum in pace with her advance. Her eyes skated over my legs, stopping at my pink panties before moving over my white camisole and up to my lips. Before she could paralyze me with another kiss, I reached around and unhooked her bra. Her breasts came free, filling my hands. Taut brown nipples teased my palms as I squeezed, trying to map every contour.

"God, Glory, that feels good."

"Your breasts are so sexy." I managed before her mouth came in for more.

My fingers rolled her nipples then traced the undersides of her breasts. She groaned into my mouth. I smiled and nipped her bottom lip. She was going to be so fun to make love with. My hands skated down her sides, taking her panties off. Her legs kicked them free. I wrenched my mouth away to look down the length of her. Lean with identifiable tone, her love of outdoor activities showed in every movement on her legs and abdomen. Dark, trimmed curls covered her core and summoned my touch.

She drew her tongue up my neck, kissing me quickly before sitting up to straddle me. Her hands smoothed over my cami down past my hips, reaching all the way to my knees. It was like she had to touch every part of me before it would be real.

"You're so beautiful, Glory."

"So are you, Lena."

I reached up and pulled on her hips. She dragged across my pubic bone, both of us moaning at the sensation. She lifted up onto her knees. My hands reached out to bring her back. She laughed and swatted them away as she busied herself with pulling off my underwear.

"You just get better and better," she whispered.

Her hips straddled me, taking her time to settle onto me. When we connected, I seized up, fighting off the urge to climax. That had never happened so fast before. Just one touch from her and I'm nearly coming.

She leaned down and kissed my mouth once, trailing down my neck as her hands went to the hem of my cami. It was halfway up my chest before I realized what was happening. My hands shot out to stop hers, redirecting them to where I wanted them most. She resisted until her fingers landed on my wetness. She let out a low curse at how excited I was.

My hands returned to her breasts, fingers sliding alongside each nipple before pulling slightly then pinching. She moaned with every tug, hinting at how sensitive she was.

The hand cupping me came back to reach under my camisole. To distract her, I flipped her over onto her back. My mouth went on the attack, trailing down her neck and chest before sucking a nipple in. My tongue lashed out, flicking up over and over. Her back arched toward me, hands gripping my head.

"Glory, please," she moaned, her hands coming back to the only remaining barrier.

I pulled her hands away and pinned them beside her head. My mouth didn't let up on her sensitive nipple. Her hands pushed against mine, but my position kept them in place.

"I want to see you," Lena said.

"You are," I responded, moving toward the other breast.

Her wrists broke my grasp. They slid down my sides, coming back to the hem of my undershirt.

"No," I told her, trying desperately to distract her with my mouth.

"Yes," she said.

"This is good like this." I leaned down and covered her completely, settling a leg between hers and barely moving to show her how good tonight would get.

"Glory," she said in a remarkably lust-free voice.

I looked up from where I'd placed my thigh and saw that her eyes had lost their sexual craze. "Let me touch you."

"Take your clothes off."

"They're off." I slid against her thigh and groaned.

Her eyes rolled back, but the distraction didn't last long. "Your shirt, Glory. I won't be the only vulnerable one here."

"You're not."

"I don't do one-sided."

I lifted up to straddle her. "Nothing about this will be one-sided."

"Then take off your shirt. I want to see you, touch you. Kiss you everywhere." Her voice held tender hope and it almost convinced me.

"We're doing just fine like this." My hands dragged down her chest, fingers splayed to touch as much of her as possible.

"We're not. Either we do this all the way or we don't do this."

"Oh, we'll be going all the way, sexy." My fingers brushed over her mound.

She pulled my hand away. "Your shirt."

"Come on, Lena. You're not really going to stop this now. Not when I've barely started with you. Not when we're both so close to coming, a breeze might do us in." I leaned down to kiss her, pouring everything I promised into one kiss.

"Don't hide from me, please." She looked both determined and vulnerable. "I've seen scars before."

I wasn't conscious of moving, but my legs swung off of her. I pulled upright and fought not to turn away. I'd been in this position before. Twice, and both times, my partner had stopped when he or she saw my chest. They'd had to be coaxed into finishing what we'd started. Yes, one had been an asshole teenage boy, but the other had been an experienced college woman who assured me that she'd be fine. She hadn't been. She'd turned off the light and avoided touching my chest. I made a decision that night. It would be the last time. I wouldn't go through that hurt again. None of my casual sex liaisons cared if I kept a shirt on.

"You've seen scars? No, you haven't. You've seen pretty little lines cut by a scalpel and sewn back together to barely mar the skin. You haven't seen a scar on top of another scar, on top of another scar, on top of yet another, and again, and oh, one final one on top of that. You haven't seen skin knitted together as a baby that then stretches to the size of a woman being opened and reopened six times. It doesn't look like the doctor used a scalpel with me. It looks like he cut me open with a chainsaw. That isn't something we need to see tonight."

She swallowed, blinking away moisture from her eyes. "It is."

"Lena." I let a disbelieving laugh escape. "You're not really going to walk out of here when we're both worked up right now. Let me finish, please."

She stopped my hand from touching her. "I'm sorry. It's all or nothing. We're equals here or we're not doing this."

I deflated. I couldn't believe she'd stop this right now. Not when she'd kissed me like she needed my kiss to live. Not when she'd responded to my hands on her breasts like she might climax just from that.

When I didn't move, she sat up and reached for her shirt. In seconds she had it on and was sliding off the bed to step into her underwear and slip on her pants. I'd never seen anyone dress that quickly before.

"You're really going to walk out in the middle of this?"

She raked her hot gaze over me, regret in her eyes. "I don't want to, but I won't have another relationship ruined by power plays." She moved to the doorway. "You know what I want. It's up to you where we go from here."

With that she walked out of my bedroom, leaving me more than just hot and bothered.

Chapter 25

Irritation flared all afternoon. For the past two days if I were being honest. Brooke and Hazel had already commented on my much shorter than normal fuse. I knew what it was, but I wasn't about to say it out loud.

How could she have left like that?

Hazel buzzed me from reception. My least favorite clients were in reception without an appointment. Just what I needed, something more irritating than my thoughts.

"Hi, Wendy, Keith, what brings you by?"

"Oh, we didn't think you'd...we were here to..." Wendy hedged.

"We'd like our file. We're switching accountants." Keith was talking to Hazel.

That shocked me out of irritation. As annoying a client as Keith was, he'd been one of the first businesses I'd landed when I put out my CPA sign. "Are you unhappy with my service?"

Wendy scoffed then looked surprised by the sound. "We're going in another direction."

Accounting didn't have many other directions unless they meant an illegal one. I gestured toward my office, but they stayed rooted to the ground. "Another direction?"

"We're not staying with you. Not now." Keith had flared up at client meetings before, but this didn't seem like a flare up.

"I can't force you to stay, but you're valued clients." If valued meant pains in the ass, that is. But I wouldn't be rude or pass up their billables just because Keith was a lot to handle.

"We're going to use Ted."

The financial advisor? They ran four very different businesses. Their tax structure was confusing to me, and I focused on taxes. Ted made commissions on stock trades. His client meetings consisted of trying to convince his clients to invest more so he'd get higher commissions.

"He's not a CPA or a tax attorney. He's not qualified to do your taxes."

"Of course he is."

I'd suffered many headaches courtesy of Keith, but I couldn't just hand them off to someone who wasn't qualified without sufficient warning. "He can assess your financial situation and recommend investments, but he is not a tax specialist, certainly not a business tax specialist."

"We're not staying with you!" Keith rippled with anger.

I stepped back. "I've been looking out for your business finances for six years, Keith. Do you want to tell me where this anger is coming from?"

"You want a reason?" he taunted.

"Keith!" Wendy raised her voice.

"Forget it. She asked for it," he barked at his wife. "You've been lying to us for years."

I took another step back. "I have never once misrepresented anything on your accounts or tax filings."

"We're not talking about our businesses," Wendy said.

"Then how have I lied to you?"

"You're a lesbian and you never told us. Do you know how much that goes against everything we believe? How humiliating it was to learn that you'd tricked us?" Keith said.

Wasn't this old news yet? Since Andy started talking, I'd noticed a few whispers and stares. Some clients had asked, but most just approached Brooke, Hazel, or Mei. I still couldn't figure out what my sexuality had to do with anyone in town. I wasn't dating them. Why did I all of a sudden go from being their accountant or friend or acquaintance to being a lesbian? It made no sense that my sexuality, which had never been front and center with me, was now the first and seemingly only label they affixed.

"I'm sorry you feel that way. If you'll settle your account with Hazel, I'll have your file copied and delivered to your office. For the record, I've never once lied to you." I turned to head back to my office.

"You're lying now."

I swiveled back, letting the irritation I'd been feeling have an outlet. "Did I ever tell you I wasn't a lesbian?"

"You've been dating the mayor for years. You dated the sheriff's son. You've been lying to everyone."

"Spencer and I have always been upfront about the fact that we're just friends. I've never lied to you about anything, especially not about something that is none of your business." I could feel my face grow hot and remembered why I tried not to let things bother me. Anger never did anyone any good. "If you'll excuse me, I have some quarterly tax filings to finish. You might want to remind Ted that he's got three days to finish yours or you'll owe a hefty fine. And when he admits that he doesn't know what you're talking about, good luck finding another tax specialist closer than Denver."

Their breathing came in quick pants as they glared at me. Hazel saved their sure retort by waving their bill and demanding payment. They wouldn't dawdle with this bill like usual. Now that they knew a deadline was looming, they'd want their file.

Idiots. I crossed my fingers that they were the only clients who felt this way. I had plenty, but I didn't like losing any for something so trivial.

I gave Hazel enough time to get their check and stamp their invoice paid. The door closed with a loud bang, and I resurfaced with my briefcase. "Think I'll leave early."

Hazel studied me. "Don't let them get you down, Glorious One."

"They're not. I'm just feeling tired and worn down. I might go home and plan a little vacation."

She sat up straighter, energized by my pronouncement. "That sounds like fun."

"It does, doesn't it? Right off the top of my head."

"I like when you go with your gut. You head on home." She waved me out the door.

Ten minutes later, I was shoving a load of laundry into the machine. I'd clean my bathroom next and think about planning a vacation. It was too hot to be sitting outside, and truthfully, I was avoiding my porch. I shouldn't be. I wasn't the one who'd walked out at a compromising moment.

By evening, I couldn't help myself. Television didn't appeal when I had a good book and the lovely outdoors. I headed out to the porch with some ice tea and the banana bread I'd made last night when I was avoiding the porch. Spencer's mower sounded in the distance, and I thought I could smell a barbeque from Nancy's direction. In front of me, I watched three squirrels leap from limb to limb in their version of squirrel tag. Definitely better than television.

"Hey," Lena called out from the street. She was struggling with the little used leashes in both hands. Kitty was trying desperately to drag her toward me.

"Hi." I waved, trying to play it cool. The last time I'd seen her, she was naked beneath me. That was a hard vision to dismiss at the moment. "Hi, doggies." They both jumped at my greeting.

Lena laughed and let go of their leashes. They bounded toward me and she lagged behind. I rubbed them, waiting to see what she'd do. It took longer than normal, but she made it onto the porch and lowered herself into her usual chair.

I turned my surprised expression back to the squirrels. "Having a good day?"

"I started putting in a few hours at school while the rest of the staff is off for July. It's nice and quiet, but sometimes spooky."

"Redrum?" I guessed, quoting the king of all spooky movies.

She laughed, which made her relax against the chair. "I think my head was playing with me today. It's amazing the creaks and clicks that happen in a large unoccupied building."

"Shouldn't you be taking your vacation time like everyone else?"

"They've been at their jobs for years. I'm still trying to make my way here."

I respected that. It wouldn't make me go in to work when I had a sanctioned and paid month off, but I respected her viewpoint.

She took my offer of ice tea and banana bread. We sat without speaking for a while. Her dogs both chomped on extra bread. After fifteen minutes with no mention of what happened between us, I began to wonder if I'd imagined the other night. Perhaps we hadn't been about to make love. Maybe she hadn't ever kissed me. By the look of us now, those things couldn't have happened. Surely one of us would bring it up.

But she'd definitely kissed me. I knew that much. I'd never been kissed that well before. I'd never been convinced that a kiss was anything more than two mouths touching. It hadn't been anything other than a pleasant addition to making love. But Lena's kiss had been like wind to a kite. Everything about it cranked me up. I'd wanted more. I still did.

Funny how pride can screw things up. I wouldn't acquiesce because I was certain I'd endure the same kind of hurt, possibly worse since I already cared very much for Lena. Yet I was still vexed that she'd been able to walk out when she didn't get what she wanted. We'd been naked and ready. The awkward, sometimes clumsy part of sex already taken care of. Only the good stuff was left to do. And she'd walked away. Made a demand, and walked right out the door. Damned if I did and damned when I didn't. My pride got roughed up that night for sure.

"Anything new at work for you?" she asked, tossing water on the flames my memory was sparking.

"My two worst clients are probably going to get audited and fined for not meeting a pretty important tax deadline. All because they didn't want to work with a lesbian."

She shifted in her chair to look at me. "I was going to ask if you'd decided to tell everyone recently. I've overhead a few conversations around town these last few weeks."

"You're out, too, you know."

She seemed startled by this. "Terry?"

"Yep."

"Is that why I can't seem to get Jennifer on the phone anymore?"

I shrugged and hoped not. Jennifer was a nice lady. I'd hate to think she was a bigot.

"Who'd you finally tell that can't keep her mouth shut?" She flicked her sleek ponytail over her shoulder, expending some of her snark.

"No one ever asked. They all assumed I was straight because I dated Rick in high school and hang out with Spencer now. Everyone who should know does."

"Why has it become a recent news item?"

"This town has nothing better to gossip about, I guess."

She continued with her questioning glance. She could be persistent like that.

"Andy. He's known since I moved back. Don't know why he's sharing now."

She scoffed again. "People do strange things when they're hurt."

I nodded and leaned down for another dog rub. She could have been speaking about the other night, but she probably meant it as is. It would explain Andy's odd behavior since his separation. I couldn't care less about his diarrhea of the mouth, but he didn't seem to be acting in a healthy manner these days. At least he wasn't holding up the divorce. It would be finalized in a week.

"We better get going." She stood and patted her leg to get the dogs up. "It's my brother's birthday. I've got to put in a call and convince him to come for a visit."

"If he's a skier, he won't be able to resist our winters."

She smiled, looking off at nothing. "I bet that's what he's been waiting for. I hadn't thought of that. Thanks."

"Any time."

She waved and headed home. I was left with a little more comfort about our friendship than I'd had over the past two days. It wasn't enough to stop the gnawing sensation from eating at my stomach. I never liked unfinished business. A move, one way or the other, had to be made.

From the Journal of Lena Coleridge:

I gave her every opportunity tonight. I made the first move by going over there. Yeah, she was shocked that I'd left the other night. Left her practically naked and so ready, but that was it, wasn't it? Practically naked wasn't going to cut it. I can't do that again. Can't let someone get everything I have to give while she keeps parts to herself. I won't be hurt like that again. If she's not willing to be completely open with me, I'm better off without her. I learned my lesson with Regina the Money Grubber. I doubt Glory would be like that, but hiding part of herself from me was all the warning I needed. Damn, I wanted her. Want her still. I gave her a chance tonight. Gave her the choice to resume our friendship or take a chance with me.

And she let me walk away. Again.

Chapter 26

Sunday night, I was restacking my depleted wood pile to ready it for delivery tomorrow. I always received deliveries in the summer. It was less expensive and they could get it out to me right away. My parents sometimes waited until November before they got their wood. It had backfired a few times, leaving them without heat from the fireplace for a couple weeks in winter.

Complete fatigue plagued me by only the fifth log. My breath came in gasps, and it felt like a small vehicle was trying to parallel park on my chest. Fleeting spasms followed by massive pressure. It was all I could do to get back into the house and lie down. I hadn't felt this kind of chest pain in years. Something had to be wrong. I didn't want to think about it, but I was adult enough to deal with it.

"Back again, Glory? I'm going to get a complex." Dr. Pickford took his spot on the rolling stool and gave me an encouraging smile when he'd rearranged his schedule to see me the next day. The chest pain had subsided, but those were always the magic words when dealing with a cardiologist.

"Apparently I can't stay away."

We went through an ultrasound. Then he hooked me up to the EKG. "Oxygen level has dropped again."

"Another stent?"

"Possibly, but I'd like to wait for the MRI results to come in."

We waited in silence while Stacy went to collect the folder from my MRI at the imagining lab this morning. Dr. Pickford must have been throwing his weight around to let me jump the line like that. She came back into the exam room with a large envelope. The doc took his time looking at the images. He turned with a heavy expression. My heart jumped, making my chest hurt again.

"It's not good news. It's your valve."

"Pulmonary?" I swallowed what felt like a large, hard lint ball.

That was the one I'd needed replaced when I was seventeen. If it was my tricuspid, that could mean a repair only. Pain and recovery on that would be minimal compared to what I was used to. Replacement was a much bigger production.

"Yes." He let that sink in. Compassion poured from his eyes. He gave his patients this kind of news every day, and still he was able to feel for them. "We knew it would need to be replaced at some point. I'd hoped it would last longer, but the good news is there have been a lot of advancements in the last ten years. You may not have to replace it ever again."

I fought against the lump in my throat again. "You think it's my valve? Not just an artery?"

He reached for my hand. "I do."

He never pulled punches with me. It was one of the reasons my family had moved from Portland to Aspen when he'd moved his practice to Denver. He had been one of a few qualified pediatric heart surgeons on the west coast. I wasn't willing to shift to the others, and my family thought nothing of moving to be near him. Ours wasn't the only family to think that way either. Several others had relocated to the Denver area to keep seeing him. We all consider ourselves stalkers.

He pointed to the valve on the image and reran the ultrasound pictures on the screen, explaining as he went. "It's the valve. And it needs to be soon."

Tears built behind my eyes as I tried to shake them off. I swallowed roughly again and tried to speak. "You have to go in again? Open me up?"

"I have to go in, yes, but it'll be minimally invasive this time. Valve advancements aren't the only improvements. I'll make three incisions and go in through your ribs."

I blew out the breath I'd been holding, not quite sure I'd heard him correctly. "You won't crack the breastbone?"

"It's possible I may have to, but I've got robotic help now. I should be able to get in through the ribs. You're still looking at six to ten weeks of recovery time, but it's less painful and less time than when you were younger."

"Okay," I tried to process that. "No other options?"

He waited for me to retract that question. He didn't like being scary blunt, but I had to know for sure. "Your valve needs replacing, Glory. If we don't, it will stop working. At that point it will be a lot more pain and maybe too late."

More pain and too late. Words no heart patient liked hearing. I wouldn't be able to ride this value until it died, hoping it might repair itself. He was telling me that my heart would overwork itself to compensate for the bad valve until it stopped working altogether. Nope, no other options.

"You'll have to decide on mechanical or tissue." He knew I'd get to where he'd been as soon as he saw the MRI. "We didn't give you that choice when you were younger for a couple of reasons. Mechanical is a good option now, and the only chance at not having to do this again. Some fail, but most last for a lifetime unlike tissue valves."

"I'll be on blood thinners for life."

"Yes, that's the drawback."

"And they click." I'd done lots of reading on the subject, knowing at some point I'd be facing this decision unless I had a miraculous tissue valve. I wasn't sure how I felt about something inside me that made a mechanical sound, no matter how soft. "The tissue valves last longer now?

"Some patients get lucky and go twenty years, some longer. At your age, you'd be looking at another two to four more replacements if you go tissue again."

"How long do I have to decide?"

"We need to get you scheduled soon. I don't like that you're having chest pain. We can't risk valve failure."

I nodded, trying to delay the feeling of being rushed. "Surgery when?"

"I can get you in tomorrow. Wednesday would be more difficult."

Not even a day. My muscles felt tight and my head pounded. Tears pushed at the back of my eyes. I wasn't ready for this. The stent replacement should have cleared me for years until the stated expiration date of my tissue valve. Two years at least. I would be prepared to make this decision and face another recovery in two years. But I wouldn't get that two years. I wouldn't even get a full day.

"Wednesday isn't good?"

"Tuesdays and Thursdays I'm at the hospital."

I knew that but needed the extra time to decide. "Tomorrow."

I found it harder to stand from the exam table this time. When I'd made the appointment I was hoping for sheer exhaustion and a lecture from the doctor about pushing too hard. I didn't imagine I'd be walking out of this room and needing to check into a hotel because I'd be expected at the hospital first thing tomorrow morning. Flashbacks of my last valve replacement recovery flooded my mind as I left the office. Eight days in the hospital followed by two months of slow recovery at home. I didn't feel whole again for another two months after that. Facing even half that filled me with dread. Of course, all of that assumed I'd make it through the risky surgery.

* * *

Coasting down the hallway toward the operating room, I held my mom's hand. My dad was right behind her, a brave look on his face. Mom and I had been giving him a hard time all morning as I signed the forms for the surgery. He seemed more nervous than both us of combined.

Dr. Pickford stopped the gurney at the double doors leading to the operating suites. He looked at my parents and told them what they'd heard six times before. "I've got your girl from here. I'll do everything I can to take care of her."

Mom squeezed my hand and leaned down to kiss me. "We love you, sweetie."

Dad stroked my shoulder. "You'll do great, honey."

I blew them both a kiss. "I'll see you soon."

The routine had worked for us every time before. It would work again, no matter how worried I was. To think otherwise right before surgery could invite disaster.

In the operating room, Dr. Pickford's masked face loomed over me. His kind eyes calmed some of my nerves. He told me to count back from one hundred by sevens. Math before surgery. Ugh. I got down to seventy-two and closed my eyes. I'd think of the next number in a second.

My eyes opened, and I tried to remember what came next. A nurse appeared and disappeared. I felt a lot more groggy and disoriented and had to close my eyes against the dizziness. Dr. Pickford was there when I opened them again. I tried to focus on his familiar face.

The nurse fluttered in and out of my line of sight, touching various machines and checking the tube in my arm. I turned my head to examine the operating room, but pain flared in my chest and side.

"You're in the ICU, Glory. You'll be here a day or two. Everything went well. You have a shiny new valve working and ready to take you to old age."

I understood the words but couldn't reconcile them with what I knew to be true. I still had to subtract seven from seventy-two before he could start with the cutting. Maybe I was dreaming already.

"You're done, Glory. You're out and done," he repeated.

This time I got it. I tried to smile but that took too much effort. I'd save it for my parents when they were cleared to visit me in the ICU. I'd thank him later, too. Right now, I needed more sleep. Coherent thoughts and feelings would have to wait until the anesthesia wore off and I could stay awake for more than a few minutes.

It took a day and a half, but I was finally using most of my mind. When they moved me to a regular room, I yearned for that just-came-off-anesthesia feeling. My new roommate talked nonstop. She'd had a quadruple bypass and seemed to be giving credence to her doctor's recommendation of a healthier lifestyle. If I wanted to be cruel, I'd guilt her about having a choice on her heart surgery if only she'd eaten better or exercised more. Neither would have helped me. Instead, I let her chatter on, not adding to the discussion.

I hurt, even with the drugs. My side blazed at any little movement and my chest ached in dull throbs. My roommate didn't seem to hurt. Not when she pressed the nurse's call button every thirty seconds, not when she used her bedpan every hour, and not when she tore the orderly's hands off when he brought her food trays. For my next heart procedure, I'd ask for a bypass instead of any of the other painful things my doctor always went for.

My parents came into the room as bypass lady was talking about her love of ice cream and how it had taken her straight to her hospital bed. They introduced themselves and tag teamed her so I could get some peace. I watched Mom get comfortable in the reclining chair next to my bed. It was going to take a tough nurse to get her to leave tonight. She hadn't been able to stay over when I was in the ICU, but she owned regular hospital rooms. Nurses didn't stand a chance.

I couldn't believe I'd forgotten how awful the whole surgery process was. From the scrubbing with special soap the night before to all the tests right before surgery, the endless forms, the heart wrenching worry on my parents faces before and after, plus all the pain, aches, involuntary narcolepsy, exhaustion, and tedium. It was all too much. The antiseptic smell, endless rotation of nurses, inedible food, and having to rely on someone for every single want or bodily function didn't add to the glamour of hospitals.

I'd experienced a whole range of emotions this time. I remembered being afraid when I was seventeen, but this time exasperation, envy, dismay, embarrassment, despair, hope, distress, gratitude, and even rage joined my fear. Happiness wouldn't break through until I was released.

Chapter 27

Pain meds made the car ride home unpleasant. No matter how many positions I tried, I couldn't get comfortable. Car sickness was no fun either, especially when the act of getting sick felt like being stabbed and beaten at the same time.

It was all worth it just to be home. Nothing felt as good as when my dad set me on the couch after being too exhausted to finish walking from his car. I felt love for this couch because it was in my house not in a hospital or beside the never ending drivel of some lady I didn't know. I'd liked my couch before, but here settled on it after a really horrible five days, I actually loved it.

Mom and Mei hovered nearby, watching me adjust my position to get more comfortable. Dad turned on the television and began bouncing through the channels, checking with me on each one to see what might be of interest. I doubted I'd be able to keep my eyes open for more than fifteen minutes but it was important to him to do something for me. Spence was just coming out of the bedrooms where he'd deposited Mom and Mei's suitcases. I loved these people. They thought nothing of taking time off work to drive to Denver and be with me in the hospital, arranging among themselves who would have which days so that I was never without a visitor for even one day. Now that I was home, they would be there for support, assistance, care, and love. I was one lucky woman.

The doorbell sounded, and Spence dashed off to answer it. If I'd had the energy, I would have been disappointed that I couldn't get in a nap before some of my friends stopped by. It had to be Brooke. She'd been checking in by phone daily while taking care of the office for us, but she'd probably want to see for herself that I was okay.

Lena appeared in my line of sight, worry and irritation in her expression. My heart started beating harder. So not good for a person just out of valve surgery. I wanted to stand to greet her, but my legs and back felt like clay. I'd be able to get up, but I didn't think I'd be able to stay up. I opted for the I'm-completely-healthy-nothing-is-wrong-I-just-feel-like-reclining-here-because-it's-comfortable look.

"You should have told me."

My parents' eyes went wide at Lena's stern tone. I think mine did as well. Nearly everyone treated me like I could crack open at any second after a surgery. At best they'd fuss over me, but no one would challenge me. No one.

"We haven't exactly been..." What? Talking? No, we'd managed that in the week after our little incident. Muddled through as if nothing had happened between us. As if I didn't know what it was like to have her body sliding against mine, mouth hungry and searching. "Besties," I finished.

"Cut that out!" she demanded. This time everyone's eyes widened.

Spence turned away, his shoulders started to shake with silent laughter. He'd been the leader of the Glory-you're-an-idiot-if-you-don't-snap-up-Lena club for a few weeks now. Mei had to pull him into the back hallway, probably ready to join his laughing fit. She thought Lena would be good for me, too. Having Lena tell me off seemed to solidify that notion for them.

"You have the nerve to hang out with me acting like nothing is wrong, knowing full well that you're going into the hospital soon." Her eyes blazed.

She wasn't kidding. She was really angry. I looked at my mom. I expected to see her chest puffing out, ready to defend me. Instead I saw what looked like admiration in her eyes, happy to let this play out.

"It was nothing." I wasn't lying. Comparatively speaking, it wasn't as bad as my open heart surgeries. And what would I have said? *Hey, I know you didn't want to have sex with me unless the conditions were perfect, but I'm headed to the hospital tomorrow, so want to drive to Denver and give it another try?*

"I don't want to hear your carefree B.S., Glory." Lena's tone made me abandon the sarcastic thoughts. "You can drop the easy going act. This was serious. Wasn't it? I don't even know what you had done, but I can tell. It's serious. You and I, we're...hell, I don't know, but we're definitely at the stage where you tell me if you're going to be hospitalized. You got that?" She looked fierce, like she might slap me silly.

"I like her," Dad tried whispering to Mom, but he sucked at whispering. They always carried across two rooms.

Lena stepped back to take them in. Anger dropped from her expression. Embarrassment seeped in. She'd only met them a couple times before. "Sorry, but your daughter just, just..."

"We know," Mom supplied with a sweet smile. "She does that to us, too."

"I'm sitting right here," I reminded them, flabbergasted by their complete support of Lena's ranting at their recovering daughter.

"Of course, dear," Mom placated me.

Lena refocused on me, stepping up to where her knees brushed the couch. She looked beautiful when she was angry. Then again, she looked beautiful with any emotion. I tried not to smile at how riled up she'd gotten. "Do we understand each other?"

That was a loaded question. I thought we did. Then she walked out at a time when I didn't think anyone would have the ability to leave. I thought I knew her, thought I could guess her actions, but she'd proven me wrong. Even for an easy going gal like me, her walking out had turned me sideways.

My throat didn't seem to want to work, so I managed a stiff nod. Pain sparked from my chest. My hand came up to press against it. Lena bent to reach for my hand, concern now erasing any anger or frustration. She pulled her hand back when she realized her touch may add to my pain.

"I'll get an icepack." Mom headed into the kitchen. "Henry, a little help?"

"I'm fine, Mom."

"She's good, Dana" Dad told her.

"Henry!" Mom ordered in a tone that always made him hop to.

Lena smiled as she watched my dad hurry into the kitchen. She waited until he'd cleared the room then knelt beside the couch to be at eye level. She watched my hand settle back between us on the couch. After a moment, she reached for it, touching lightly until I squeezed hers in return. "Are you well, truly?"

"I am or will be, yes."

"You look tired and in pain." She was being kind. I looked pale, ashy, exhausted, limp, and like I hadn't groomed myself in a week.

"Thanks, you look ticked and worried."

"I am, dammit." Her eyes narrowed. "Don't do that to me again."

"Yeah, because my heart condition is really about you."

That dragged a reluctant laugh out of her. She shook her head and squeezed my hand again. Her other hand slid partway up my arm. The touch felt better than being able to sit on my couch after nearly a week. "When I ran into Spence yesterday and he told me you were in the hospital, I wanted to wring your neck for not telling me."

"That probably made you more mad than me not telling you." I guessed and her eyes widened. Guessed right.

"Don't do it again. We're friends. You need to let me know when you're going through something like this."

"Noted," I acknowledged her worry and need for reassurance.

"Need anything from me?" she asked, glancing back at the conspicuously empty rooms.

A kiss, a hug, her body wringing pleasure from mine. I definitely wanted those things but couldn't possibly go through them right now. Not that I'd get them even if I hadn't just had surgery. It would be up to me to give her what she wanted. As sure as I'd been that she would relent, I was beginning to think she wouldn't.

I wondered if my expression showed any of those thoughts because she hesitated before accepting my, "Thanks, I'm good."

A smile lifted the corners of her mouth. "I'll check in tomorrow."

Why did that seem more like a threat than a promise?

From the Journal of Lena Coleridge:

My God, she looked like she'd been dragged by a bus. Wiped out, hurting, fragile, and so beautiful. I wanted to wrap her up and take the pain from her. When she wasn't around all week, I was worried and angry and hurt that she hadn't told me she'd be gone. She didn't have to tell me where she was going, just that I wouldn't be seeing her on my dog walks for a week. Sure, it's been strained at times. Always is when you see someone naked and it doesn't work out, but we've been moving back toward normal. Then she disappears and stupid me thinks it's because she was still holding that night against me. If I hadn't run into Spencer on my walk last night, I might never have known.

Hearing she was in the hospital tore me up. Flat out. Yeah, okay, obviously I care about her. I never would have fallen into bed with her if I didn't, but I nearly punched him when he wouldn't tell me specifics. Surgery on Tuesday, she'd be back today. That's all he said when he figured out she hadn't told me herself. Frickin' loyal jerk.

At first I was so angry that she'd shut me out like that. We almost had sex. We were getting so close, and she thinks she can just go have surgery and not tell me. How can she make me want to shake her and kiss her at the same time?

It was such a relief to see her back home, safe, out of surgery, hopefully healthy now. I'll find out what she had done. She has no choice in that. She will tell me. If it's something to do with her heart, I know it's a touchy subject, but she's my friend, dammit. I'm helping her through this. It didn't escape my notice that her parents and her two best friends were there. Well, she just got a new best friend. No more driving off to Denver to have surgery and not tell me. Whatever her recovery needs, I'm going to be there.

Chapter 28

Regaining my strength turned out to be harder than I remembered. Not being seventeen probably had something to do with it. Day by day, though, I was able to increase my stamina. Three weeks out, I could now manage grooming and cooking for myself. Independent again, I never realized just how much it meant to me.

Still, it was nice to have my mom pop over for breakfast or dinner and to help tidy up. Spencer came for lunch twice a week and Mei stopped off every night after work. Ashlyn had become a semi-permanent visitor, taking care of yard work and making light grocery runs for me. Brooke and Cassie came just as often. My other friends, acquaintances, and some clients stopped by with get well cards and wishes. I'd gone back to being known as the one with the sad heart condition. I wasn't sure if that was better than having my sexuality as my headline.

A tap on the sliding glass doors had me turning from my makeshift desk at the dining table. One thing about being homebound, I wouldn't get behind on my work. Lena stood outside, dogs by her side. I felt a smile pull my lips wide. My other daily visitor, Lena had definitely surprised me. Yes, she'd come by almost daily prior to my surgery, but now she never missed a day.

"Hello," I greeted all of them when I went to the door.

"We're off for our walk. Join us?"

After the first couple of days, she'd stopped asking how I felt. She just seemed to know as if she'd been there with me as often as my mom or Mei after these things. Even Spencer and my dad still tiptoed around me most times. Others would have asked if I felt up for a walk, but not Lena. She knew I had to walk a mile a day. She showed up mid-afternoon almost every day to drag me away from my work.

"*General Hospital* is on." I gestured to the dormant television in the living room.

She laughed and pulled on my arm. I winced at the stretch. My chest still ached and the incision area would be sore for another week or so. Lena noticed and immediately dropped my arm. "Sorry."

"Slight twinge, nothing big."

We started off the porch, walking at a pace that was about half my normal speed. She never minded, adjusting her stride to match mine. When I needed to stop or sit, she stopped or sat with me. If I needed a crutch in the last two hundred yards to make it home, she'd offer her arm for support.

"Will you tell me sometime?"

I called out to Kitty so he didn't get too far ahead of us on the street. "About what?"

She glanced at me then watched Kitty race back toward us. "What you had done."

"Boob job."

Laughter spilled from her lips. "Captivity has messed with your brain."

"What? Did they botch it?" I joked, glancing down at my barely B-cups.

Her eyes dropped, and my nipples betrayed me, tightening under her gaze. What I'd meant as a joke had treaded into serious territory. "They're perfect." She waited two beats and finished, "I assume. I was denied that pleasure, you'll recall."

Whoa, had she just brought up our almost night together? And joked about it? "There's the sass I've missed. I wondered how long you'd keep treating me delicately."

"I haven't been—" She cut herself off when she caught my smile. "Punk."

As we passed the Crane's house, the door opened. "Hello, you two. Glory, how are you feeling?"

"Fine, thanks, Nancy."

"Anything we can do for you?"

"Thank you, but no. I'm all set. Say hi to Calvin for us. Enjoy your evening." I waved and continued at the same pace, encouraging her to drop it. She took the hint and said her goodbyes before heading back inside.

"How many of those do you go through a day?"

"The first week, everyone I know in town. It's tapered off since."

"I've heard lots of concern. As your neighbor, I've gotten calls every day."

"Tell them I got sick of this town and moved."

"How long would that rumor take to make the rounds?"

"Resident relocation is better than affairs on the gossip scale around here."

She chuckled, coming close enough to brush against me. "Tempting. I do like messing with people sometimes."

"Really?" I asked, all innocence.

"Punk," she muttered again. "Not today, then."

"Today for what?"

"Finding out about your surgery."

I stopped myself from repeating my earlier joke, but only because talking about our almost but not quite night together was only slightly scarier than talking about my heart condition. "New valve." If we were going to be real friends, I couldn't keep pushing her away.

Her step stuttered. She reached down and stroked Fender to cover it up. "You had a heart valve replaced?"

"Yes." I took advantage of her pause and stopped for a rest. I'd made it a hundred feet father than yesterday before my first stop.

"That's serious." She blinked several times. "Major, I think."

"Avoid it if you can."

She shook her head, exasperated. "Don't do that."

"You're new to this. Come visit me in the cardiac wing next time and you'll walk away with a book full of morbid humor."

"You're already planning to go back?"

"Hope not."

She gave a single nod. Turning around, she started us back toward our houses. "Me, too. This worried me. I can't imagine how scared you must have been to go through it. You're very brave."

To go through a life saving procedure? I wouldn't call it brave, but it was nice of her to say. "Thanks."

"Please don't keep me in the dark if it happens again."

"I have to go to the dentist next month."

Her hands rose toward my neck, twisting together to mimic wringing it. "I'm serious. I care about you, Glory. We," she paused and waved her fingers between us, "care about each other. Keep me informed, please."

I heard a faint click of my new mechanical valve in the quiet between us. After three weeks it was becoming more difficult to discern the sound. Mom and Mei assured me that they couldn't hear it. But at Lena's confession, I felt and heard how rapidly the valve was working. For the first time since the surgery, the sound felt really good. Or maybe it was learning that Lena hadn't completely distanced herself from me or what we could have together.

* * *

"Hey," I called after knocking on Spencer's door and letting Mei and myself in.

"My two favorite people," Spence greeted, walking in from his back deck.

I could smell the grill going already. Trout if my nose was working right. He'd gone fishing with my dad and his buddy James last weekend, and Mei and I were going to be eating the spoils.

He smiled, his eyes flaring at Mei before swooping in for a kiss. "Hi, sweetheart."

My heart warmed at their embrace. It seemed like the second the divorce came through, their happiness increased tenfold. They were still keeping it private, at least for another three months, but they were no longer careful to seem like they were mostly associated through me. Brooke and James had also been let in so that they wouldn't have to hide their obvious affection for each other in front of the two other people they spent the most time with.

He turned and gentled an arm around me. "Sixty percent?"

I smiled at his way of asking how I was doing. "Sixty-one."

"Excellent. You can wrap the corn in tinfoil. Mei, salads and veggies, please."

"You just asked us over to cook for you," she snarked.

"I had to kill the fish, my lovely, and clean them. They require constant cooking supervision, the delicate things."

Mei laughed, pushing him back onto the deck. I loved seeing her this happy.

"Hey," I said, stopping him. "Is that a goatee? Spence, you stylish dude, when did you make that change?"

"I had a shaving mishap. Took an extra swipe. Had to bring it down to a goatee. You like? Irresistible, right?"

We both laughed. Spence could be a funny ham when he put some effort in. Mei leaned up and kissed his now bare face. He did look good and a little closer to his thirty years, too.

"Did you want to invite Lena?" Mei asked as we took up our assigned tasks in the kitchen.

"She's out at the Ducky Derby with Kirsten and Rod today." I leaned back and asked Spence through the French doors, "How'd you manage not to be there, Mr. Mayor?"

"I put in an appearance earlier." His tongue peeked out as he slid the spatula under one of the trout to flip it over.

"Slacker," I teased.

"She might be home by now." Mei insisted.

"I'm sure she's tuckered out."

"A whole day without seeing her? How will you manage?" Mei's brown eyes sparkled.

"She walked me this morning." Her early arrival had surprised and delighted me. I figured she'd skip the day with the Derby festival.

Mei nodded, a teasing glint in her eyes. "Are you ever going to tell us what happened with you two? Spence about swallowed his tongue when he realized she didn't know you'd been in the hospital. Seems like something you'd tell the woman you spend many evenings with."

"Are you asking her?" Spence said as he rushed in from the back deck.

"Stop it, you guys."

"We're curious. The way she reacted when you got back and the fact that she's visiting every day says something about her."

"She's a good neighbor?"

"No one's that good a neighbor," Spence said. "Something happened, right?"

I shook my head not about to get into the details of a failed lovemaking session with my two best friends. "She has hang-ups about my age and us being neighbors, and I have hang-ups about us being neighbors and…" I let it drift off.

"Ditch the neighbor worry. It's not like you can look out your window and see her brushing her hair in her room. You've got like an acre of trees between you." Mei scooped the now sliced veggies into a pan.

"The age thing can't be that much of an issue," Spence said, handing the cooking spray to Mei. "She fits in with us just fine."

"That just leaves whatever you're hung up about," Mei said like she was checking off line items on a to-do list.

"We're friends. It's working for us."

They gave me a long look, testing to see if they could push me farther. Mei nodded and headed out to the grill to use the burner for the veggies. Spence followed but stopped at the door.

"Rick is a dick. You know that, right?"

I snorted. "Yeah." Spence had a way of summing people up.

"Good, because I'd hate to think he's messed with your head even now that you're a mature, thoughtful woman."

Rick hadn't been the only one, though. "Not as much as you messed with his face."

He laughed, thinking back to the beating he delivered. "Okay, just thought I'd mention it."

I reached for his hand and squeezed. His concern felt good, misplaced, but good. Mei wasn't sawed in half, so he couldn't really speak to how someone might react and if that could have lasting impressions. Whatever it might be, I was still deciding if moving past the age thing, the neighbor thing, and the friendship thing only to be met by something that had ended two relationships before was worth the effort and potential awkwardness. Right now, it felt good enough just to be friends, and it seemed that Lena had come to the same conclusion.

Chapter 29

No matter how much I assured her I was fine, Lena insisted that she drive me to Denver for my follow up doctor's appointment. My parents and Mei had been insisting, too, so I knew someone was coming with me. At about eighty percent, I could make the drive on my own, but all they could see was my still slow gait, twinges of pain, and abandonment in the middle of certain physical activities. No one was sure I could make the round trip without getting tired. I'd considered flying and having Christine pick me up and drop me off, but with everyone on my Glory Watch crew willing to make the road trip with me, I thought I would take advantage.

My mom was all set to go yesterday, but after having dinner with the crew, I somehow found myself in a car with Lena. She mentioned having a friend in Denver that she could visit during my appointment time, which meant the trip wouldn't be wasted for her.

Once we got to the doctor's office, she pulled into a parking space and killed the engine. I turned to stare at her. I'd expected that she would slow down just enough to push me out of the car without major injury.

"You don't have to stop. I'll call when I'm done. Don't rush back or anything."

"I'm coming in with you." Lena was already getting out of the car.

"That wasn't the deal."

"I'll wait till you go back with the doctor."

"Lena."

"Glory," she said in the same tone. Her hand reached in through my open door to get me moving. "You're always telling me how easy going you are. Just go with this."

"But," I said to her back as she walked ahead of me up to the office door. What could I do? Drag her out of the doctor's office and throw her back into her car?

She took a seat in the waiting room as I went to check in. A magazine lay open on her lap when I came to sit beside her. I tried to think of some argument to get her to leave. I didn't like feeling uptight about having her here. There was no reason to be; especially not now that she knew more about my heart defect than most of my other friends.

Jeffrey, the staring contest silver medalist, was sitting across the way and spotted me almost as soon as I sat down. His annoying mother, who couldn't seem to stop calling his name no matter how well the kid behaved, thankfully didn't see me. Without words, we went into a stare down. Him with a huge smile and large bulging eyes and me with a relaxed posture and almost sleepy eyes. That was the key to winning staring contests.

"What are you doing?" Lena whispered, leaning into my space.

"I'm taking this kid to task."

"Mature," she murmured and went back to reading her magazine. Or pretending to read her magazine. Prior to my stare fest with Jeffrey, I'd noticed her darting eyes taking in everything.

"Jeffrey!" his mother exclaimed when she noticed him staring at me.

He broke the stare when she yanked on his head to get him to face forward. He looked back just in time to catch me crossing my eyes at him. Despite his mom's chastising, he giggled.

A nurse appeared in the doorway and called his name. I swallowed a lump when I noticed the slow way he stood and his careful steps to the doorway. It was an all too familiar gait. I sent up a silent prayer that he was already in recovery like me.

He looked back and waved with a sweet smile. I patted my heart twice and gave him an encouraging thumbs up. The least I could do was assure him that some people went through similar heart problems and came out all right. Mostly all right, anyway.

"You have an admirer, I see." Lena had put down her magazine. She watched as two other families came in the door.

"Jeffrey's cool."

"Do you pass each other notes before all appointments?"

"Don't you have a friend to visit?"

Her mouth stretched wide. "Am I bothering the only person I've ever met who never seems bothered?"

"No," I grumped, not happy that she sounded rather proud of herself.

"Glory," Dr. Pickford's nurse, Stacy, greeted from the doorway. When she saw I wasn't alone, she added, "Would you like to bring your friend back?"

"No," I said as Lena said, "Yes."

I faced her as we stood, placing both hands on her arms. "No, thank you, but no."

Lena considered me for a moment then relented. She dropped back into her seat and flipped open the magazine again.

I watched in confusion. "I'll call when I'm done. It shouldn't be longer than a couple hours."

"I know. I'll just finish this article. Call me when you're done."

With another long look, I turned and followed Stacy back to Dr. Pickford's office. She was in a perky mood, talking about her weekend plans. She'd recently gotten divorced and was looking forward to her first date in eleven years. I let her yammer on, assuming she was happy to have someone to speak with who wouldn't want a lollipop from her when the appointment was over.

She showed me inside and pointed out the gown. I was beginning to hate that gown. I'd worn one like it too many times this year. Not having a choice, I stripped off my shirt, undershirt, and bra and put the thing on.

"Hey, Glory," the doc greeted when he came into the exam room. "How's the new valve?"

"Working."

"That's what we look for in a good valve."

"Could I really ask for more?"

"Like having it zap all the cholesterol from your arteries?" he guessed.

I leaned back on the table and watched as he attached the electrodes to my chest. He did this easily and with no fuss, almost like he was brushing a piece of lint off my shoulder not staring at my bare chest spoiled by the vicious looking, wide pink scar dividing my torso. He bent to check the three new incision scars on the side of my rib cage.

"I believe some doctors in Estonia are looking into that."

Keeping my mind off what he was doing, I asked, "How are the winters in Estonia?"

"About like here without the wonderful ski resorts or award winning heart surgeons." He stood back and attached the electrodes to the EKG machine to run the first test.

"Awards? Am I being charged more now that you've won awards?"

"I've always had awards, and you're one of my favorite $3,000,000 women."

Despite knowing I had to stay still for this test, I choked at his figure. I knew he'd just pulled it off the top

of his head, but thinking back, it wouldn't be hard to
come to that number given the now seven heart
surgeries I'd gone through with two valves, one shunt,
four stents, and annual monitoring. Cardiac surgeries
these days were equal to the purchase price of a home in
a city. These tests weren't cheap either. Thankfully, my
dad had chosen his health insurance option well before
I'd been born. A small co-pay for everything while the
insurance picked up the rest. I should feel guilty that I
was one of the reasons health care was so expensive for
people. They were not making any money on me. Then
again, my dad had paid premiums his whole life and he
rarely went to the doctor.

"Everything sounds and looks good on that one," Dr.
Pickford interrupted my thoughts on the current health
care status in this country. He turned back to reach for
the wand and gel for the next test.

My shoulders lifted off the table when he squeezed
the cold gel onto my chest. The wand pressed down and
glided over my skin. Images of my heart popped up on
the machine. Pulsations turned the light shades lighter.
He'd once shown me what a normal heart looked like on
an ultrasound. The difference was remarkable between
a heart with four functioning chambers and mine with
one side working and the other not.

He watched the monitor with no comments. He liked
to do that. Like it was a game to keep me in suspense.
"Valve is clicking away."

"Yeah."

"Does it bother you?"

"Sometimes I'm really aware of it, but probably
because I've been tuned in to my recovery. My friends
tell me they can't hear it. I'll just have to get used to it."

"Good." He clicked off the machine and took the
wand away. Stacy handed me a wipe and headed out of
the exam room. "Things are progressing nicely. I'm

clearing you for everything but aggressive physical activity."

"Fight Club is out?"

He turned back from writing in the chart and smiled. "Definitely. No sex for two more weeks either."

"Won't be a problem," I muttered, pulling my gown back together and sitting up.

"Really?" His brow rose. "Stacy mentioned someone sitting with you in the waiting room."

"Stacy has a big mouth."

"You should hear her gossip about my six-year-old patients. One of them wouldn't share his toys with his sister in the waiting room just yesterday."

"Scandalous."

"The someone?" he insisted, not letting up. He had asked about my work and hobbies and friends all throughout my life. He liked to keep abreast of my life. One more thing that made him a great doctor.

"A friend."

He patted my arm and stood. "I'll see you back in three months." He headed to the door and turned before he left. "A little love will do your heart good, Glory."

"Thanks, Dr. Phil."

"That's sarcasm, right? I don't get much of that with six-year-olds." With that he left me alone to get dressed.

On my way out, Stacy put a hand on my shoulder to stop me. "She's pretty."

I felt my brow knit. She spotted my confusion and tipped her head toward the waiting room. I leaned to look around the wall and through the reception window. Lena was sitting in the waiting room. I checked my watch. An hour and a half had passed. She'd sat out there waiting for me.

"How long have you two been together?"

I felt like telling Stacy that I'd only just realized her name was Stacy not Sydney. It might make her doubt she had the right to pry into my life. It wouldn't be kind, though, not when she looked so happy to be talking about grownup stuff. "We aren't. She's my friend. See you in three months, Stacy."

Lena looked up when I came through the door. She dropped her magazine onto the table and stood without a word. We fell into step together heading toward the elevator.

Out in the parking lot, I asked the obvious because it just didn't make sense, "You waited?"

"I had to catch up on all the Hollywood breakups."

"Brad and Gwen?" The doc's magazines were seriously out of date.

"It's shocking, isn't it? I thought they'd last forever." She unlocked the doors and we got into her car. "You must be hungry. You'll like my friend Barb. She's going to meet us at the restaurant."

If I weren't starving from fasting before my appointment, I would probably protest busting in on their reunion. I couldn't pass up lunch, though.

She made her way back into the city without once checking her directions. She'd probably had time to memorize them waiting on me. Driving past the Brown Palace hotel, she headed toward Union Station. When she parked, I had a good idea we'd be eating at the old brew pub around the block.

Before she got out of the car, she turned and asked, "Healing nicely?"

I liked how she'd waited almost twenty minutes to ask. "Everything's fine."

"Fine as in you'll be able to climb Snowmass Overlook with me this weekend?"

I laughed at the idea. "That's always going to be out of my range unless you want to give me a piggyback ride for most of it."

She reached out and grabbed my arm. "What? I thought...shouldn't a valve replacement be like new after you've recovered?"

My brow furrowed until I realized that she'd gotten her initial information from Jennifer, who only knew I'd had a heart problem that required surgery back in high school "The valve was only one of my issues."

"You mean the other three might need to be replaced?"

"The other one that functions hasn't given me a problem yet, but I'm down to two chambers and a rerouted vascular system to compensate. I'll never have the energy or stamina that you have."

Her mouth nudged open, concern filling her eyes. "I shouldn't have taken Jennifer's word for anything. I'm sorry for being so insensitive."

"You didn't know. Most people don't." I looked down at her hand on my arm. "Thank you for coming with me today and for waiting. That was very kind of you."

"You mean a lot to me, Glory. Next time, maybe I'll muscle my way into the exam room with you."

A thesaurus of emotions rolled over me. Fear first that she'd see me so exposed, ending with exhilaration that perhaps my doctor had been right.

Chapter 30

Despite winning district last year, the volleyball team didn't have a lot of support for their games. Brooke, Mei, and I were there to watch Ashlyn and Brooke's daughter, Izzy, in their first game of the season. I always tried to catch one of Ashlyn's games for every sport that she played. Her teams weren't always great, but she was an incredible athlete.

While the team was warming up, I spotted all the mothers of the kids on the team. More than half were my clients. I waved to each as they found their seats and did what everyone did in a small town, looked around to see who else was here.

Footsteps sounded from behind coming down the bleachers. A hand pressed down on my shoulder as Lena settled into the space next to me. She'd said that she might be at the game, but I felt my stomach flutter at the sight of her. "Hey, guys. It's great that you're supporting the kids."

"Mandatory for me," Brooke groaned. She didn't like sports, but her daughter played three well. She was in for another two years of sporting events.

"You don't fool me, Brooke," Lena teased her. "You'd watch Izzy knit for two hours if that was her thing."

I was happy to see that they'd become good friends since their first meeting at my house. Lena had been keeping to herself and work for the first couple of months in town. Now she was more social with plenty of residents and friends with quite a few. While it took her off my porch more often, I was glad that she was getting more ties to the area with these friends.

Ashlyn headed back to the bench with the team after warm-ups. She looked up and spotted us, waving wildly, knowing we'd come to see her. I was eager to see if the summer camp improved her already impressive skills.

"I don't know how good she was last year," Lena said about Ashlyn, "but I've peeked in on their practices and she's very good."

"She's been varsity since freshman year."

"I can see why."

Brooke elbowed me and nodded her chin in the direction of my former clients, Keith and Wendy. Their son was in the band and being excessively rich, they spent a lot of time hovering over him. Their faces swiveled back around as soon as my gaze hit theirs. They waited three beats before turning back to see if I was still looking at them. I could feel the condescension laser through me as their gazes bounced from me to Lena. What idiots.

"I, for one, am glad they dropped us."

"They dropped me, Brooke. You were just swept up in the wave. I am sorry you lost their business."

Lena tilted to look down at them. "Those the bigots?"

While uttered at a whisper, I still looked around to make sure no one overheard her. She was speaking the truth, but in a small town it wasn't a good idea to make enemies. As the principal who would be in charge of every kid in town, she definitely couldn't afford to anger the locals.

"The former clients, yes."

She gave me a full wattage smile at my politically correct phrasing and rubbed my arm. Someone gasped behind me. We turned to see another of my clients staring at us.

"Glory," the woman greeted then immediately looked away.

"Rumors," Lena murmured. "Just what I need."

"Welcome to a small town," Mei sighed.

"Celebrate them. That's what I did when David and I first got together," Brooke said. "We started more rumors about ourselves than anyone in town. It was fun to hear all the conflicting stories running around and see what the folks did when they heard the complete opposite of the rumor they'd been spreading."

"Twisted pup," Lena accused.

"I collected some of those rumors," Mei said. "I thought I'd compile them and have them made into a little book for Brooke and David's twentieth anniversary."

"Illustrated?" Brooke kidded.

"Graphic novel," Mei shot back.

Mitch and his son skated along the bleacher in front of us. "How are you feeling, Eiben?"

I tipped my chin and smiled. "I'm well, thanks, Mitch." Very close to a hundred percent and looking forward to no more heart issues for a long time. Gone now was the constant nagging in the back of my mind at the knowledge that I'd eventually have to have my tissue valve replaced. Without that worry anymore, I felt incredible.

Several others followed Mitch's precedent and asked after my health. It took ten minutes before I finished with the inquisition and was able to turn back to my friends.

"How's she doing? Such a poor thing. She doesn't deserve this," Mei mimicked in a low voice.

"Sweet girl. Too bad about the heart thing," Brooke added.

Lena stared wide eyed at their joking nature. She hadn't gotten to the comfort level of ribbing me about health problems yet. I just hoped she'd stick around long enough to get there.

"You're not going to stroke out before you finish my tax return, are you?" I reiterated the best one I'd heard in all my time in town.

"What?" All three of them asked.

"Sensitivity-challenged Billy posed that one during tax season this year. He apparently heard about my stent procedure but wanted to make sure I finished his taxes first."

"Moron," Brooke snorted.

"I don't think I've had the pleasure," Lena commented then turned to me. "Stent procedure?"

"Uh," I started, wondering if she'd yell at me again. "You'd just moved to town."

Her eyes scorched mine. "Book club week?" She didn't wait for my confirming nod. "I knew something was going on that week."

"She keeping things from you again?" Brooke teased. "She does that. You'll get used to it."

"Brooke," I said, exasperated.

"Won't happen again, right?" Lena asked. It wasn't a question.

"Go, Izzy!" Brooke yelled suddenly as the team sprinted out to take their positions, ready to start the game.

"And she doesn't like sports," I joked to Lena.

She smiled and brushed her shoulder against me. "I'm glad you're here. It's so much easier to avoid parents when I've got a friend around."

I was, too. What started out as a support night for Ashlyn turned into a fun evening with friends. The possibility that one friend might be something more just added to the enjoyment of the evening.

Chapter 31

We'd spent the evening on Lena's deck. Another barbeque, this one attended by our friends, neighbors, and my parents. That Lena hosted was yet another step to cementing her stay in town. More and more people would stop her around town just to chat. She was becoming a real local.

"We're helping, Spence," Mei was telling him as I went back onto the deck after clearing plates.

"I've got it covered, guys. Head home. Thanks for coming." Lena gestured them off the deck empty handed.

I looped my arm through Mei's and started off the deck with her. Lena gripped my shoulder after two steps and, still making polite noises to Spence and Mei, managed to keep me in place.

"This cookout was your idea, missy. You're helping."

Spence turned and walked backward throwing me a gloating look. He always got out of things in town. Everyone thought the mayor was too busy for the trivial things that made life go round. Little did they know he had a very good staff and worked efficiently. More nights than not he was home before me.

I watched the front door close behind them, leaving me as the last party guest. "It was your idea."

"You're always saying I should invite people over and get to know the town."

"That doesn't mean this was my idea."

A ghost of a grin drifted over her face. "You were going to offer to help anyway, so get over it." She tossed a towel at me.

"I'll wash." I tossed the towel back at her because I knew it would irk her just a little to have her plan slightly disrupted.

It didn't take long, our system now locked in place after many dinners together. The ease of motion around each other felt great. I'd known Brooke far longer, but I didn't feel nearly as comfortable in close proximity to her. That should tell me something.

We took some wine into the living room after cleaning up. It was an unconscious motion. We didn't have to think. We just grabbed the open bottle and two glasses and headed into the living room. I knew I was welcome. That I could stay as long as I wanted.

"That was fun. I really like Brooke and David."

"I can tell. She's needed a good friend for a long time."

"Needed?"

"Yeah. She's been a workaholic since I've known her. It's only recently that she's started to do more than just take care of her kid and work. Now that Izzy is older, she's been on Mei and me to go out more. With you around, Mei and I don't have to babysit as much."

Lena chuckled. "So really I'm just a convenience for you?"

"That's about right."

She pushed against my shoulder and I rocked sideways and back. "She's a wonderful lady and becoming a good friend. I'm glad you introduced us."

"I am, too." I took a sip of wine and sighed, relaxing into the couch. It no longer scared me how comfortable I was around her. Not much scared me about her anymore.

Except being pushed aside by someone else. *Holy...*I can't believe that just occurred to me. She wouldn't stay single forever. She wasn't like me. Just because I'd been willing to wait her out didn't mean that she'd do the same with me.

"What's up? You look like you just had an idea."

I did. I reached forward, resting my fingers against her face.

She tilted into the caress then seemed to remember she shouldn't be doing that. "Don't start this, Glory. Please."

I noted the desperation in her voice. She was fighting the pull, too. Well, forget that. I leaned in and brushed against her lips. Even this little kiss set me aflame. I slanted my mouth to deepen the kiss. She accepted me, and her body tilted against mine. My tongue slid along the seam of her mouth, teasing her before breaching inside.

"Oh, damn!" she whispered, pulling back. "We can't do this. I don't care how good it feels." Her eyes were dilated and her chest heaved. She was as wrapped up as I was.

It might have been the sizzle from her kiss or the encouragement from my friends, but I made a decision. I decided to have faith that she wouldn't be like anyone else, that she wouldn't hurt me. In what felt like slow motion, I brought my hand up and began unbuttoning my shirt to take it off. If her eyes had shown anything but complete surprise, I wasn't sure I'd continue. Any hint of smugness that I was giving in might have made me leave.

"Please tell me you're not going to stop," Lena said as my shirt hit the floor.

I shook my head, too nervous to speak. She tugged on our hands and I followed to her bedroom. It was the first time I'd seen it and as with everything Lena, it was elegant.

My hesitation must have worried her. She cradled my face and kissed me softly. "Are you sure you're ready to give me all of you?"

I'd been with other women before, but this felt deeper. Almost permanent. "You said all or nothing, Lena. I wouldn't be here if I weren't sure."

A lovely smile spread her lips before they came down on mine again. My hands went to her shirt, unbuttoning without hurry. I wanted to savor this. My fingertips brushed against her skin as the shirt came open. Soft and warm, it seemed to jump in the wake of my graze.

Her hands were drifting over my shoulders and onto my undershirt, sliding down my back. She pulled me tight against her, leaning into our kiss. When she moaned, I felt a zing flare through me.

I had her pants over her hips, pushing blindly to get them off her legs. She broke away to help me, stripping them down and kicking them off. While she was there, she unfastened my shorts and shimmed them off my legs. Her urgency was one of the sexiest things I'd ever seen.

When she looked back up, one eyebrow rose as if to question what I was smiling at. It made my grin wider. At the same time, I stepped toward her and nipped her chin. She laughed before tilting to capture my mouth again.

My hands drifted around to unhook her bra. Those gorgeous breasts I'd tried so hard not to remember were inches away from me again. I pressed a hand to her neck and slid down her sternum to cup one breast then the other. She moaned again and whispered something I didn't catch.

Her fingers hooked under my cami and began to lift it up. She pulled back to watch as she revealed more and more of my skin.

I searched her eyes, worried even though I knew I shouldn't be. She wasn't like Rick or Maggie. We were closer than I'd been with any of my sexual partners. When the undershirt cleared my belly button, her eyes blinked once. As it rose to reveal more and more of the surgical scar that had been stitched together, stretched as I'd grown, and reopened five times, her eyes started to shimmer.

The cami off now, she unhooked my bra and let it fall. She tracked my scar from sternum to waist and slowly back up again. Her eyes landed on my breasts, flaring before rising to look at me. "You're perfect, so beautiful," she whispered.

Her hand pressed onto my heart, applying pressure to gage my heartbeat. Fingers drifted over and traced my scar. It was the most tender caress I'd ever felt.

"Thank you," I whispered and reached for her.

Pressing against her, I maneuvered her onto the bed. Crawling over her as she inched up toward the pillows. She looked amazing stretched out before me. Long limbs, smooth skin, lust filled eyes. Where to begin? My mouth and hands and eyes wanted everything of hers. I wanted to feel her warm skin, watch her nipples harden, kiss her belly, and taste every part of her.

A soft chuckle sounded as she leaned up and took my mouth. Her hands latched onto my head and encouraged me to explore. I ran my tongue down her throat, nipping along the way. Her legs fell apart, relaxing completely. I pressed a knee between them, straddling one thigh as my mouth kissed and nipped my way down to her breasts.

She was so responsive. Even more so this time than last. Like she'd been holding back before, but with a couple more months of getting to know each other, she knew she didn't have to hold back anymore. My heart seemed to swell in size at the realization. I felt a little dizzy and had to slow down to see if it was the euphoria of being with her or the exertion of being excited.

"No hurry, Glory."

I glanced up to see her watching me. She didn't look worried. She only wanted me to pace myself if I needed to. "I want you so much."

"I want you, too," she agreed, lifting up to kiss me while she could.

A moment later, I felt her hands pushing me onto my back. I stared up at her as she examined me again. When her eyes hit my panties, her eyebrows fluttered. An instant later, I was completely naked and laid out for her viewing. She seemed to be taking her time.

Finally, her hand glided from my belly up to a breast, squeezing softly before sliding back down and dipping into me. We both moaned at her touch. My hips arched up toward her, encouraging without words. Her fingers slipped over me, outlining then mapping out. I felt breathless but not dizzy. It was hard to concentrate until I figured out that I didn't have to. I could let her do anything to me. I didn't have to worry that she'd get too close or want too much from me. I would give her anything.

"Stop teasing," I growled when her fingers again missed my clit.

"Stop directing. You'll have your turn."

I wanted to wipe that superior grin off her face when she went back to torturing me. Only one way I could think of to do that. I lifted the thigh that was between her legs and rubbed against her wet panties. Her whole body bucked, and sure enough, the grin dropped.

She sucked in a breath, pulling her hand from me to shed her underwear. The break in contact must have given her senses back. With deliberate movements, almost like she was creating a show for me, she centered herself back onto my thigh. It tingled where she seeped onto me. The soft trimmed curls felt incredible as she jerked her hips once.

"Damn, you're wet." I waited for her eyes to meet mine, lifting up from watching herself slide against me.

"Like you aren't?" she teased, her hand dropping back to cup me fully. "You made us wait for this."

"It'll be worth it," I groaned as I felt her fingers finally brush against my swollen clit.

My thigh muscles contracted against her. I set my hips in motion to wring a climax from her. My hands clamped down on her hips, forcing them against my thrusting thigh. She took over the motion, freeing my hands for her swinging breasts. She looked so sexy, grinding on top of me. I pinched and twisted her nipples, remembering how much pleasure she got from the sensitive peaks. I'd been determined to make her come before me, but damn if her fingers weren't making me forget my determination.

She swirled my clit lightly, applying alternating amounts of pressure to drive me into a frenzy. Her eyes peered into mine. "You're going to come for me, Glory."

I felt her weight shift from my thigh. She wasn't moving against me anymore. No matter how far I tried lifting my upraised thigh, she wasn't allowing me enough contact. It seemed she was better with determination.

Her finger sped up, pressing a little harder. When her mouth lowered to my breast, sucking then licking, I felt the anticipated tingle start. No one had ever touched or kissed my bare breasts. Damn, I'd missed out. The tingle burst into a flare, wild and hot, revving through me before exploding with roiling pulsations. I heard myself shout, making the climax real. My body twitched as the orgasm ran through every part of me.

"You're amazing." Lena watched every movement of my recovery.

I gulped in breaths, letting the bliss of orgasm settle across me and tried to calm my racing heart. For once I wasn't worried that my elevated heart rate would make me collapse. I didn't care.

She stretched out against me, resting a leg over mine and stretching her arm across my chest. I tried to collect my thoughts and gain control of my nerve endings. She seemed content to let me lie here for hours, not demanding anything. Her lips brushed against my neck, fingers playing with my nipple.

When I regained my strength, I turned onto my side to face her. Kissing her first, my hand drifted down her body to delve into her. She hissed sharply, so close to the edge. I nudged my leg between her thighs to add extra pressure.

Her eyes opened and stared longingly at me. I'd seen that look before and always wanted to act but hadn't been ready. I couldn't be happier that I'd moved past my hesitation. Her hips rocked slightly. My fingers spread her apart, grazing every slick and puffy surface. Her clit throbbed under my fingertip. I brushed upward then down, tracing the hood and flicking the knot of her. She moaned loudly, pressing her face closer to mine. She watched my eyes as I made love to her. Our bodies rocked together, one hand holding her close to me, the other extracting her orgasm.

I watched her eyes pinch shut as she shattered around me. A long groan spilled from her lips before her eyes fluttered open again, fixing on me. Lust long gone, replaced by an emotion I guessed she'd be shocked to see on herself. It kicked my heart rate into a higher gear.

"You look so sexy when you come." My words broke her emotional gaze.

She blinked and smiled. Her arms snaked around me, pulling me tighter. "I could kick you for making me walk away from that."

Laughter burst from me. Of all the pillow talk she could utter right now, a threat wasn't what most women would want to hear. From her, though, it was exactly right.

She kissed me to stop my laughter but ended up joining me as we cuddled in post orgasmic bliss together. I loved the feel of her warm body against mine. I could have her again and again and never be bored.

"You're staying." She popped up onto an elbow to stare me down.

My eyebrows rose. "I'm staying," I repeated.

"I was telling you. In case you were thinking you had a choice."

I let another laugh slip. She was so good for me. Uptight enough for the both of us. "I left my medication at home."

Her head tilted. "You take it at night or in the morning?"

"Before I go to bed."

She nodded and started to get up. I reached out to keep her in place, but she broke free. "Come on, slow poke. We'll take the dogs for a walk to your place, get your pills, and head back."

"Because I'm staying?" I teased.

"You're not leaving tonight." That wicked grin was back. "I'll kick you out tomorrow."

We grinned together as she began throwing my clothes on top of me. I got caught up in watching her as she began to cover her gorgeous body. I would never guess it was ten years older than mine. She was in fantastic shape.

Seeing that she was almost completely dressed, I started pulling on mine. She seemed to be in a hurry to get to my place so we could come back here. The fire in her eyes told me we weren't finished tonight. I felt my breath push out at the thought of having her again. I'd taste her this time.

She opened the bedroom door as I was stepping into my shoes. The dogs raced inside, whining and demanding attention. The scene was so domestic. It would have frightened me before. Now, I soaked it in.

Domesticity, something I'd never allowed myself to think about before because of my heart condition, now seemed like the only goal in my life. Damn, that sex must have catapulted me into an alternate universe.

Chapter 32

Warm and still sleepy, I stretched before opening my eyes. It was bright, like the blinds weren't drawn, and these sheets were softer than a baby chick's fur. I had to get some of these sheets.

"You're awake," Lena's morning voice sent a shiver through me.

I tilted my head to look over at her. She was propped up on an elbow, smiling at me. Her tousled hair fell over her shoulders, skirting the brown tips of her nipples. What a sight to wake up to.

She reached forward and ran her fingers through my hair. It was a familiar feeling like she might have been doing that before I woke up. "Taylor was right, very soft."

My hand felt for her hair, half stroking the strands, half rubbing her breast. "Yours, too."

Her eyes dropped to my hand, watching it get bolder. She shook her head and smiled. "Frisky in the morning, huh?"

"Around you, anytime." I shifted until I was half on top of her. She was so warm and soft, even better than her sheets.

She watched me, a sly smile animating her lips. Her head lifted up, mouth meeting mine. Soft lips nipped at first then fused into a full, mind scattering kiss. Searing, steamy, and minty. Minty?

"You brushed your teeth! No fair," I screeched pulling back and clamping a hand over my morning breath mouth.

Her laughter filled the room. "You took a while to wake up. I had time to pretty much memorize every inch of you."

Horrified, I flipped onto my back and pulled the sheet up over my head. I heard her laugh again and felt her tug at the sheet.

"Hmm, something else that bothers the laid-back chickie from next door. This has been an eye opening morning in every possible way."

I folded the sheet down to glare at her. It was hard to stay irked when she was having so much fun. "Payback, sexy, payback," I promised.

She raised her brow and inched her hand down my neck, pulling the sheet back as she went. "I'll look forward to it." Just as she was about to caress my breast, she stopped and poked my nipple. "Day's wasting, Glory."

I watched her vault out of bed, noticing she'd put on panties in her devious pre-wakeup duck into the bathroom stint. I could have stayed in bed for another couple of hours, especially with her around. Looks like I didn't have that option.

A finger tooth scrubbing and hasty dressing later, I headed into the kitchen. She'd found shorts and a tank top and was now rummaging through the fridge. The dogs had been let out of their den as she called it and danced around with biscuits, running back and forth between us.

"Grocery day." Lena closed the fridge empty handed. "Hope you can wait for breakfast."

I was about to make a suggestion when the phone rang. We both stared at it. She didn't want to be rude, and I didn't want her to miss a call. I tipped my head for her to answer it.

"Hey, Eri," she said when she picked up the receiver. "Good, yeah, but can I call you later?"

I couldn't hear her sister's voice but enjoyed the sheepish smile that came over Lena's face.

"Nope...when we talk later...you already know who."

This time I heard a loud screech through the phone. Lena pulled it away from her ear, laughing, but the voice continued to shout. I made a guess and gestured for the phone.

"Good morning, Erika," I said into the receiver.

"Glory! I'm so happy for you both. Are you happy? You better be happy!"

I laughed. "Very happy."

Lena's eyes grew warm and sparkled. It was all I could do to concentrate on finishing the phone call and not attacking her again. Saying goodbye, I handed the phone back to Lena who made speedy work of getting her sister off the phone.

She came over and wrapped her arms around me. "I like you happy."

I squeezed her tighter and stole a kiss. That made two of us. "But you can't feed me."

She pulled back and looked guilty. "Dog biscuit?"

"Lucky for you, I live close by and I'm stocked with coffee cake and eggs."

She made a noise that sounded like she would eat my arm if I didn't take her to where the food lived. I watched her dart off down to her bedroom and the water flipped on in her bathroom. The dogs and I played ball for maybe three minutes before a sparkly clean Lena came back into the kitchen. Her hair was tied back and she had on fresh crop pants and a sleeveless polo. A three-minute quick change with shower. She must be really hungry.

The dogs burst out the door ahead of us. I slipped on the shoes I'd left by the door and followed them out. Not two steps later, I felt her hand slip into mine. I looked up and saw her smile, getting confirmation that I wasn't the only happy one in this new arrangement.

The morning sunshine warmed me almost as much as the memories from last night. It felt liberating to walk this familiar stretch with a familiar person but connected this time. I didn't want to drop her hand ever if I were being truthful. It was probably just the newness of the whole thing making my mind crazy, but I'd ride out the euphoria as long as I could.

I let us in to my house. The dogs scampered ahead, sniffing through each room. Lena would have followed them but her nose already knew where the kitchen was. It took two minutes to warm up some coffee cake for her and start the coffee. She waved me off to a shower, telling me she could handle making some eggs.

My shower lasted longer than hers. Drying off, I glanced in the mirror. Stupid grin aside, it looked like my skin was glowing. The scar that usually made my eyes skip across to find something else to focus on didn't look as red or ugly this morning. Not when the incredible woman who'd been making my heart flutter for months didn't even falter when she looked at me. Studied me, touched me, and made love with me without one moment of hesitation. I'd been wrong about how it would go, and it never felt so right.

"You sleep in, you take long showers, what else are you lazy about?" Lena teased when I got back to the kitchen. She was just finishing the scrambled eggs, having already set out plates for us. The coffeemaker chimed, and she almost skipped over to pour some into mugs.

"You wore me out last night, and I had to wash my hair. That's the drawback with fine hair. You of the Thick & Luscious Clan can probably go a couple days without washing yours."

Her eyes roamed over my wet hair, a grin on her face. She took a long sip of coffee and shuddered as the caffeine hit her system. "Three days sometimes, and for this coffee and cake, I'll let you laze away a whole day if you want."

"Oh, you would?" I slinked over and pushed up against her. Another shudder ran through her body, this time without the caffeine. My whole body flushed with heat that I could do that to her.

"Perhaps. What did you have planned for today?"

My arms reached around her, stroking her from her neck to her perfect ass. "Nothing planned, but lots of options. Spence, James, his dad, and my dad are going fishing. My mom, Mei's mom, and Spence's mom are headed to Eagle for some festival or another. Brooke is taking her daughter and Ashlyn for a tour of the campus in Boulder. And Mei—"

The front door opened and Mei's voice called out, interrupting me. She walked into the kitchen and came to a sudden halt, seeing me in Lena's arms. "Oh, sorry to barge in."

Lena looked down at me. "You were saying about Mei?"

I stepped back and said hello to my friend, trying to assuage her embarrassment at storming in on us. "She was going to stop by this morning to see if I wanted to visit Cassie's new colt."

Lena laughed. "Morning, Mei."

"Hey, Lena." Her eyes darted to mine, a huge smile on her face. She'd be grilling me the first second she got me alone. "I'll be knocking from now on." She looked at Lena. "Damn glad I finally have to."

"Hey!" I objected, but it did make me look like I wasn't a slut in front of Lena.

"We can see the horse some other day." Mei started backing up.

"Sounds fun," Lena said, turning to pull another plate from the cupboard. "Had breakfast yet?"

I tried not to look surprised at how she was taking things in stride this morning. Almost as if we'd switched personalities last night. Or perhaps I was rubbing off on her.

Mei gave me a questioning glance but when I tipped my head in encouragement, she took the last stool at the counter. "You're up for seeing the new colt?"

Lena looked at me then Mei. "Never seen one before."

I tried to gage if she was being polite or if she really thought spending part of Sunday looking at a two-day-old colt would be fun. Her unwavering gaze told me she was looking forward to it.

Mei nodded and flipped open her phone. A second later she was telling Cassie we'd be coming by after breakfast.

I took the moment to lean in and ask, "Thought you were going to kick me out today."

Lena smiled wide, lowering her head for a soft kiss. "Today's not over yet."

No, it wasn't, and I'd be savoring every last longitudinal rotation of the earth today.

From the Journal of Lena Coleridge:

I'm so screwed. Last night was, hell, I can't even bring myself to say it. I'll sound like a bad romance novelist. An unpublished romance novelist, so sappy and clichéd I can't even get an online site to publish the bad prose. I knew this would happen. I knew it would be amazing—she would be amazing. Just kissing her is the stuff of fantasies. Better than any fantasy I conjured up. The whole night, it just, and the number of times she made me—God, I really can't say it.

Then spending the day together, getting to touch her whenever I wanted, kiss her all day, imagine her laid out on my bed. So beautiful, everything in perfect proportion to her lovely small frame. And those scars, the ones she wanted to hide from me, I could worship them all night knowing they were there so that she could be here with me.

So now I'm screwed because, dammit, she's mine. Not about to tell her that yet. She likes making me crazy. She'd take that little nugget of knowledge and do everything in her power to torment me. Stupid, stupid me. Should have just slept with her in that first month. Quick and unemotional. But no, stupid me, had to get to know her, get to care about her, want to spend time with her, crave her friendship, and then sleep with her so the only possible outcome is—nope not going to say it. I'm not there yet. I'm not! But I am screwed.

Chapter 33

Three weeks into the new school year, the extracurricular clubs at the high school held a carnival. Even if the board hadn't been invited to attend, Ashlyn, Izzy, and Maddy had all stopped by the office to get Mei, Brooke, and me involved. Brooke and David would be building their booth and games, Mei would be getting her mom to make her spring rolls on sight, and I would bake and bake and bake.

In between using every oven on my street, I typed up my resignation letter for the board. I'd offer it to Terry at the end of the carnival. The need to resign had grown since the last meeting, but now that Lena and I were together, it became urgent. She'd tried to discourage me from quitting, not wanting to make me change anything about my life now that we'd become much closer. After a week of debate, she began to see things my way. I couldn't be in a position of authority over her.

The soccer, softball, baseball, and track fields were teeming with people by the time I showed up. Ten bucks later, I'd gained entrance to the carnival. I spotted Cassie and her husband right away, their two small kids already sticky with cotton candy. Many other parents from the school board meetings waved hello as I did a tour of the booths. The kids had done a creative job this year.

"Glad you could make it, Glory." Kirsten stopped me in my perusal of the kids' booth.

"I didn't have much choice. You've got some pretty savvy negotiators at your school."

She laughed, nodding her head. "They are persuasive."

"Have you seen Lena around?" I tried for casual and think I pulled it off.

"Two of the games were having structural problems. She was dragging David over to shore them up last I saw." Her finger pointed off toward the far end of the lane.

I thanked her and headed in that direction. I wasn't sure if Lena had told Kirsten about us, but she had a knowing smile on her face as I followed where she'd pointed.

"Glory!" Ashlyn's voice called out from my left.

I looked over and found her standing in front of a plywood shelf system with stuffed animals ready to be toppled over. A long line of kids stood ready to throw the softballs. Ashlyn was the money taker and barker, getting more and more kids interested.

The booth beside her stood out with bright colors and creative decoration. It also looked the most professional of the ones I'd seen. David really was a master handyman. Four tiers were filled with my cakes, breads, cupcakes, and cookies, all with price tags equal to an upscale coffee shop. An equally long line stood waiting to hand over money for a small taste.

"Looks great, Ash," I said, drawing up to the side of her game table.

She didn't miss a beat, taking the next contestant's money, explaining the instructions and handing over the three softballs that a teammate of hers was stacking from the missed attempts. "Doesn't it? Maddy thought of everything. Did you see the other game?"

I glanced over on the other side of the booth and found a ring toss game, manned by Izzy and a couple other teammates. I waved as she took in the money from the next gamer. "Popular booth."

More than popular, actually. It had twice the number of people waiting to play or buy than any of the other booths I'd passed. I felt proud of these kids, the three girls especially.

"Your stuff is selling like mad," Ash told me. "Some dude bought one of your cakes for a grand."

My eyes popped wide. I knew it was part fun, part fundraiser for the clubs, but it was a lot to plunk down that kind of money for a cake even if it supported a great cause.

"Hey, Glory," Maddy came out from behind the booth. "Did Ash tell you?"

"Sounds like you guys are doing great."

"Yeah, you've got to meet the other kids in the club." She dragged me back to meet the other four kids. They all gushed and thanked me for contributing to their bake sale.

"You know my parents, right?" Maddy pointed to her mom and dad, who were helping Mei's mom with the spring rolls.

"Wonderful to see you again, Glory." Maddy's mother was her twin, just older.

When Maddy's attention got pulled away, her father leaned in. "We'd like to thank you for talking to Maddy. We could feel her pulling away, and I don't know if she would have had the courage to tell us what was bothering her if she didn't have some support."

I smiled, happy that Maddy's stress had evaporated. She'd been pretty shy when Ashlyn brought her by and we all talked. I encouraged her to make a decision to tell her parents or not. One way or the other, she couldn't stress anymore. It wasn't good for her health. I learned through Ashlyn that her parents had been relieved when she'd come out to them.

"Ashlyn is the one you want to thank. I was happy to listen, but Ash is your daughter's biggest supporter."

They agreed and flashed big smiles when Maddy came back to tell us all about how much their booth had made so far. It sounded like a lot to me.

"Glory," Terry greeted when he came across me. "Heard you had quite the summer."

I frowned and wondered what gossip he'd been listening to. Terry loved being in the thick of things around town. When reporters from travel magazines wanted tips on where tourists should go to feel like a local, they called Terry much to the chagrin of many locals.

"Are you feeling okay?" he asked.

I nodded, understanding now. I hadn't run into Terry at all this summer because I'd spent eight weeks mostly homebound. "I'm well, thank you for asking."

"Worried us a bit, you know. We don't like to hear about your ticker giving you problems."

"Me, neither, Terry."

He laughed and leaned over to pat me on the back. Jennifer approached us with a problem parent. She gave me a tight lipped smile. I wasn't sure if my health status this summer had made her uneasy around me or if it was something else, but she hadn't called even once. Normally, she'd be good for a movie or dinner a few times over the summer. Maybe Lena's guess had been correct.

She suggested that we grab Mitch and Joel for an impromptu board meeting to address this parent's concern. Just what I wanted at a carnival. Nothing spells fun like a board meeting.

It took a few minutes before we found Mitch and Joel and a table where we could all gather. I could feel the resignation letter so ready to pop out of my pocket before anyone even said a word. Terry encouraged Katie, the problem parent, to speak.

"I would like to know," she started, and I settled in for another of her diatribes. She used to be one of my clients years ago, but since marrying a rich doctor who wintered in Aspen, she'd switched to his accountant in Denver. She glanced over her shoulder in the direction of Maddy's booth and continued, "what this board is going to do about getting rid of that club?"

Our eyes followed her bejeweled finger as it pointed to Maddy's booth. Five kids were chatting happily with the customers, selling them baked items, and handing out brochures about their club. To their left and right, the girls from the volleyball team raked in dollar after dollar on their fun games.

"Why would we want to do that?" Terry asked.

"Don't you see what it is?" Katie said to him. "What do you think those letters stand for?"

"What do you think they stand for?" Joel asked.

"I had to look it up online. LGBT means gay."

"It means lesbian, gay, bisexual, and transgender," I corrected.

"You'd know," Katie snorted as she all but ignored me.

"I would," I confirmed, causing different reactions from everyone at the table. Andy's mouth must have stopped yapping once he finally signed his divorce papers. It didn't look like everyone had been clued in quite yet. "And so should you. It isn't some secret society; it's a well known acronym."

"And you're fine with that?" she asked Terry. "It might as well be a gay sex club."

"Really, Katie," Mitch scoffed at her.

I looked over at him, surprised that he'd spoken up. He didn't normally comment in meetings, but especially not with Katie. They apparently had a bad history.

"Lena," Terry called, catching her as she was walking by.

She stopped and turned toward us. Her eyes took in everyone, casual professionalism in place. She looked exactly as a principal should look at an extracurricular activity: dressy jeans, nice blouse, minimal makeup, and casual hair in a French braid. Her eyes inched wider as she saw us gathered together, but she sat in the offered chair with a quick glance at me.

"Tell us about the LGBT club," Terry asked her.

She nodded. "It's one of six new clubs this year. They've been doing wonderfully tonight."

"Katie seems worried that it might be, what did you call it?" Joel flicked his gaze at Katie. "A sex club."

Lena was so cool, she didn't even laugh. I knew she'd think this was as ridiculous as I did, but she was better prepared for ridiculous parental rants. "No sexual activity will take place at any of our clubs, Mrs. Stafford."

"They play chess in the chess club. What do you think they're going to do in the gay club?"

"These students want a support system." Lena said. "Chess players like to hang out with other chess players. Homosexual and bisexual students want to know that there are other people like them at school. High school is hard enough. They don't need to be completely ostracized because of their sexual identity."

"But it's about sex!" Kathy demanded.

"No, it's about sexual preference. I don't see you objecting to the abstinence club."

"That's different."

"All the clubs are different, but they all have one similar goal: to provide support to like minded individuals."

"This shouldn't be allowed." Katie told Terry.

"These kids need the support this club provides. They need it. If it helps prevent even one kid from becoming another tragic statistic, it'll be the most important club at this high school." Lena spoke calmly, despite the tension I spotted in her shoulders. She had more patience than I thought anyone could have.

"I can't believe the board allows the district to spend money on extracurricular activities like this."

As treasurer, I spoke up. "That's what this carnival is all about. The faculty advisors are not paid overtime and any activities or competitions the clubs want to take part in are self-funded."

"What teacher is going to want to lead this, this...club?" Katie insisted.

"I am," Lena's strong voice left no room for argument. "And for the record, that booth has already brought in twelve times more than any other booth tonight. Since all the money goes into a pool, they'll be mostly responsible for funding the activities of all the other clubs."

"If there's interest and we have faculty support, I don't see anything wrong with any of the clubs here tonight," Terry said, glancing again at the popular booth. "And Lena is capable of running any of these clubs."

I felt Lena turn fully toward Terry. I tried not to look at her because I knew she'd be as shocked as I was by Terry's full support.

"I still think—"

"Thank you for your comments, Katie," Terry cut her off. "This is a carnival. I think it's time we enjoyed the fun."

I glanced at Lena as everyone broke and headed out to have that fun that Terry talked about. A sweet smile played across those lips that had been driving me wild for two weeks now. If I were being honest, they'd been driving me wild since I'd met her. Damn, she was fine.

"I'll be back in a minute," I said and left to corner Terry alone. "Terry, do you have a sec?"

"What's up, Glory?" He stopped his advance to the bake sale.

"I wanted to let you know that I'm resigning from the board."

"What? No. We need you on this board. You're the only one that can keep all the finances straight. Sometimes you're the only one with a voice of reason."

"Well, thank you, but I've been doing this for three years, and I think it's time."

"The school year just started. You can't leave now." He reached out to literally hold me in place. "I know the last couple of meetings have been tense, but it's an adjustment period. Lena is doing a terrific job, but she's new, an out of towner. As soon as everyone gets to know her, these meetings will go smoothly again."

"It's not the tense situation. I'm not comfortable being in a position of authority over many of my friends. It's time for someone else to step up and serve her time on the board."

"I can't stop you, but will you stay on until we can find someone else?"

"One more meeting. Two months should give you plenty of time to find someone else." I shook his hand and said goodbye.

I found Lena talking to some parents next to the Spanish club booth. They had huge smiles, gesturing back to the kids helping the ones swinging wildly at the piñata. More satisfied parents, clearly. She was so good at her job it was almost dazzling.

"How did he take it?" Lena asked when the parents wandered off.

I felt a smile take over my face. I'd tried to remain stone faced while at the impromptu board gathering so I didn't show preferential treatment, but I didn't have to hide that now. Her matching smile made my heart thump. "Tried to talk me out of it."

"Of course."

"I caved."

Her eyes went wide. A second later she laughed and pushed against me. "You evil little punk."

"But you dig me."

She blew out a loud breath. "I do."

She wanted to kiss me. I could read her mind, but she was at work and all the kids and parents kept her discreet. "Come on, we'll get some corn on the cob and check out more booths. We'll save dessert at the bake sale for later."

"Will we?" I liked to give her a hard time about her incessant planning.

She smiled, a promise to torture me later. "Yes, because you dig me, too."

I did. A lot.

Chapter 34

Sunday afternoon, a gang of my friends were walking through Snowmass Village, enjoying the relatively tourist free area for the first time since Lena moved here. We planned to walk the nature trail and picnic along the way. I'd mentioned our plan to Mei and Brooke at the office, and they'd jumped on board, bringing in Brooke's husband and daughter who invited Ashlyn and Maddy. Mei got Spencer lined up and her dad who called my dad. Cassie and her family were on board, too. We were fifteen total, strolling through the Village, intermittently breaking off into smaller groups to explore here and there.

I looked over at Lena, who had become more easy going around large groups in recent weeks. It was a big relief to me because I came with a lot of people baggage. For a woman who moved partway across the country on her own, stepping into a relationship with a woman who had a lot of ties may be intimidating. Thankfully, she'd become great friends with Brooke and David, and she really liked Mei, Spence, and my parents. When I'd told her that our Sunday hike would now be hauling thirteen others, she didn't even blink an eye.

We got stopped many times on our way to the deli. Locals learned to cherish this time between Labor Day and the start of the ski season. We'd reclaim every part of town, even the tourist traps. It was great to walk through town and recognize most of the people we passed.

"I'm getting roast beef," Dad told me as we entered the deli. "Don't tell your mother."

Lena and Mei's dad laughed. I just shook my head. My dad was starting to put on a little weight now that he was in his late fifties, and my mom was constantly worried about his cholesterol levels.

"I'm getting some spring rolls," Mei's dad declared, making Mei and I gasp. Her mother's spring rolls were the best. He was committing sacrilege.

Lena came over to stand behind me as everyone squeezed inside. I felt her body brush against mine as we all took turns ordering. She'd been making me crazy with our time together since we'd first made love. She'd stop by after work for a drink on the porch almost every night, but she'd usually go home afterward without once getting naked. She saved that for a Friday or Saturday night. I'd liked the slow before, but now it seemed like a game to her. See how much she could wind me up before vanishing.

Her hand came up to grip my waist as she leaned forward to give her order. Any contact was titillating at this point. A sound of surprise came from my left. I turned to see Jason, one of my former classmates, staring at the placement of Lena's hand before shooting his wide eyes up to me.

"Uh, hey, Glory," he managed.

"Hi, Jas," I said to his retreating back as he sprinted behind the counter to get back to work.

"Yet another friend?" Lena asked.

I twirled to face her, grabbing her hands and bringing them to my hips. "One of Cassie's ex-boyfriends. Mei and I were forced to be nice to him."

"Not really a friend, then?" Lena glanced over my shoulder at him. "He seems mighty interested for not being a friend."

I stepped closer and rested my hands on her hips. "He's hoping that I make out with you in front of him, I'm sure."

"He's hoping to see a lot more," Spence guessed from his spot closest to Lena.

Mei elbowed him and sighed in sympathy at us. "Ignore him."

"Honey," my dad called out from the other side of Brooke's family. "Do I like the mac or potato salad here? Your mom always orders for us."

"You're having neither if you're going through with the roast beef threat. Get a Cobb salad with vinaigrette."

"This is my day of freedom," he grumbled, but I noticed he ordered the Cobb salad.

Once out on the trail, it didn't take long before I was completely worn out. Wrangling fifteen people through the afternoon had been a lot more work than managing the trail by myself. We turned back shortly after the picnic, and it wasn't too soon for me.

Lena and I ended the day on my porch. Her dogs settled into their spots as I collapsed into my chair.

"You're tuckered out." Lena noticed as she sat with me. "Was the hike too much or just a long day?"

"I'm starting to think your solitude thing might have something to it."

She smiled and ran her hand down my arm. "I'll make you a loner yet."

I leaned toward her, tilting my face up. She took the hint and closed the distance, kissing me like we had hours to do nothing else. Her lips had this way of infusing energy into me. I no longer felt exhausted.

Breaking the kiss, I got up to shift over to her chair. Setting my knees on each side of her lap, I put myself in a better position to kiss her. I took my time exploring her mouth as my hands drifted over her. She moaned, spurring me on. I wanted her naked. Right out here.

Before I could get her shirt over her head, she stopped me. "It's a school night, Glory."

"So?"

"We're taking this slow, remember?"

"We have been."

"Two nights in a row isn't slow." Her eyes sparkled with satisfaction.

Last night had been wonderful, but I really, really wanted her again. "After more than a month, yeah, it is."

She cradled my face in her hands. "We're going to do this right, Glory."

"Aren't we already?" I frowned.

She kissed me once, long and deep. "We're doing this slowly because I want this to be the last time I ever have to do this again."

I blinked, settling back on her lap, letting her words sink in. "Last time?"

She nodded, looking at me with that unspoken emotion that made my heart do gymnastics. She was falling for me, which was a good thing because I was on the same slope with her. "The last time I ever have to start a relationship."

Warmth spread through my body at her words. She wanted to do this right. Take it slow so that it would last for a lifetime. "Sounds perfect," I confirmed.

Last for a lifetime. A goal I never knew I had until I'd gotten to know her. If I'd known that I'd get a life mate out of my neighbor when I first met her, I might have brought over more baked goods to welcome her to town.

Wasted Heart - Attorney Austy Nunziata moves across the country to try to snap out of the cycle of pining for her married best friend. Despite knowing how pointless her feelings are, five months in the new city hasn't seemed to help. When she meets FBI agent, Elise Bridie, that task becomes a lot easier.

Imagining Reality - Changing a reputation can be the hardest thing anyone can do, even among her own friends. But Jessie Ximena has been making great strides over the past year to do just that. Will anyone, even her good friends, give her the benefit of the doubt when it comes to finding a forever love?

Uncommon Emotions - When someone spends her days ripping apart corporations, compartmentalization is key. Love doesn't factor in for Joslyn Simonini. Meeting Raven Malvolio ruins the harmony that Joslyn has always felt, introducing her to passion for the first time in her life.

Blessed Twice - Briony Gatewood has considered herself a married woman for fifteen years even though she's spent the last three as a widow. Her friends have offered to help her get over the loss of her spouse with a series of blind dates, but only a quiet, enigmatic colleague can make Briony think about falling in love again.

Full Court Pressure - The pressure of being the first female basketball coach of a men's NCAA Division 1 team may pale in comparison to the pressure Graysen Viola feels in her unexpected love life.

Finally - Willa Lacey never thought acquiring five million in venture capital for her software startup would be easier than suppressing romantic feelings for a friend. Having never dealt with either situation, Willa finds herself torn between what she knows and what could be.

CPSIA information can be obtained at www.ICGtesting.com
Printed in the USA
LVOW040921081211

258358LV00001B/124/P